DANGER DOG

OTHER BOOKS BY LYNN HALL

DANGER DOG

LYNN HALL

CHARLES SCRIBNER'S SONS / NEW YORK

Copyright © 1986 by Lynn Hall

Charles Scribner's Sons Books for Young Readers
Macmillan Publishing Company
866 Third Avenue, New York, NY 10022
Collier Macmillan Canada, Inc.

Printed in the United States of America
First Edition

10 9 8 7 6 5 4 3 2

Library of Congress Cataloging-in-Publication Data
Hall, Lynn.   Danger dog.
Summary: Having failed once in the past to show responsibility as a pet owner, thirteen-year-old David is determined to save a dangerous Doberman pinscher by deprogramming him from his attack training.
  [1. Doberman pinschers—Fiction.
2. Dogs—Training—Fiction. 3. Responsibility—Fiction]   I. Title.
PZ7.H1458Dal 1986   [Fic]   86-13914
ISBN 0-684-18680-2

1

It was the first day of Easter vacation, a fragrant sunny April day when most boys David's age were outdoors doing something, anything, at top speed.

David Purdy was unaware of that. He was where he wanted to be, in an empty back row of the smallest of the courtrooms in the Johnson County courthouse. Today's cases were routine, nothing to draw an audience, so David's company comprised just a handful of involved people and a few local reporters. No one was expecting drama this morning, not even David.

Still, this was his favorite place to be on days when his father was in court and David didn't have school. He'd brought a paperback mystery to read during the boring times, but even when he was immersed in the book he still liked the feel of this room, its familiar small noises and smells. He liked the feeling of privilege when the uniformed guard at the door winked and motioned him through with a jerk of his head. He liked the richness of the carved railings up in front, and of the fluted walnut judge's bench with the rippling flags behind it, Iowa and America.

Sometimes David squinted his eyes and saw himself up there behind that bench, in black judicial robes,

1

pondering the evidence and making decisions that altered lives. Usually, though, when he squinted his eyes he saw himself within his father's form, standing at the defendant's table with his sheaf of papers before him, swaying the judge, or a jury, with his clever arguments. Always, while he listened to the cases being argued, David played all three parts—prosecuting attorney, defense attorney, judge—argued both sides, and then made his decision. For David Purdy this was the most exciting kind of head game, better than television game shows or surprise quizzes in school, because it wasn't a matter of knowing one correct answer. Anyone could memorize facts. The thrill was in taking known facts and manipulating them into a useful defense or prosecution, in digging down under the known facts to find the human reality of the situation.

At thirteen David Purdy was obviously his father's son. He was tall for his age and heavy-framed, with a softness of shape that forewarned of weight problems later on. He had sun-streaked blond hair and thick, pale eyebrows lighter than his skin in summer, and large brown eyes that gleamed with intelligence.

David's father Nathan was cut from the same bolt of goods, as Grandmother Purdy was fond of saying. Nathan sat now at the defense table, with his back toward David, his large shoulders hunched over his notes. A circle of pink skin shone through shaggy pale hair, a bald spot that seemed to grow larger every time David looked at it. Nathan's neck and jowls were thick and most of his suit jackets failed to meet, button to buttonhole, over his belly. David didn't see details like that, though; they were too familiar. He just saw his father, and felt invisible connections between himself and Nathan.

"All rise," the bailiff called, and David closed his book to stand with the others in the room as the judge strode in, swirling his robes. David imagined how that would feel, all that heavy robe material swirling around his legs and arms, and the whole roomful of people standing at attention when he made his entrance. He smiled, thinking that if he ever wore judicial robes he'd always walk fast enough to make them billow like that.

". . . court, in and for the county of Johnson, now in session, you may be seated."

David sank back but didn't reopen his book. This was the case he'd come especially to watch, and he'd paid for the privilege with a sixty-block bike ride. This was the dog case, and he wanted to hear all of it.

The plaintiff was being sworn in, with some difficulty because his entire left arm was thickly bandaged and in a sling. There was also a sizable bandage on the man's left cheek and ear. The judge instructed the man merely to hold up his right hand, never mind about placing the left one on the Bible. The man swore to tell the truth, then mounted to the witness chair and sat, wincing.

The plaintiff's attorney asked gentle questions. "Can you tell us exactly what happened on the afternoon of April second?"

"I was doing my job."

"You work for Old Capitol Soft Water Service, is that right?"

"Yes, sir, I'm an Old Capitol service man. I call on

3

my customers, service their water softeners, add salt, and so on."

"Go on."

"Well, Mr. Jacobson there, he's one of my customers, and I was going—"

"Mr. Jacobson. The defendant in this case."

"Yes. Him, over there."

"Go on."

"Well, I opened the side door, to go down in their basement where their unit is, their water softener, and their dog attacked me."

"Had you done anything to provoke the attack?"

"No, sir. I just went in the door and the dog nailed me right there on the landing. I yelled bloody murder, you can imagine, and Mrs. Jacobson, she come tearing down there and pulled the dog off me."

"And then?"

"I passed out. I guess Mrs. Jacobson and some neighbors got me to the hospital and that's all I know."

"Now, you're sure you did nothing to provoke this attack? Nothing that the dog might have construed as threatening?"

"No, sir. I was carrying a fifty-pound sack of softener salt on one shoulder. I couldn't very well have started nothing."

"I see. Can you tell me what kind of dog it was, about how big a dog?"

"It was a Doberman pinscher, I'd say seventy, eighty pounds. A big one, all muscle. And meaner than hell."

"Objection," Nathan Purdy said.

"Sustained." The judge nodded.

The attorney went on. "Mr. Phelps, had you ever seen this dog before, or had any contact with him?"

4

"I'd seen him, sure. Usually he was tied up out in the yard, and I always made sure to stay way clear of him. Them Dobermans can be dangerous."

"Objection," Nathan said, but without much hope, and the judge replied, "Overruled. Go on."

There were more questions, mostly repeating the information already given. David could see what the attorney was doing, establishing that his client, Mr. Phelps, had been merely doing his job in his usual way, and that the dog's attack had been unprovoked. David sat forward, curious to see how his father would weaken those facts.

Nathan Purdy stood and began his questioning. It was brief, dealing mostly with establishing the fact that dog bites were a known and accepted risk in Mr. Phelps' work, as in any job that required going onto private property when the owner might not be at home.

Then Mr. Phelps stepped down, and Nathan's client, Mr. Jacobson, took his oath and climbed into the witness chair. Nathan questioned him.

"Can you tell the court under what circumstances you purchased the dog in question? Max, is that the dog's name?"

"Yes, sir. His registered name is Von Hoff's Maximillian. We call him Max."

"And why did you buy Max?"

"Our neighbor's house got broken into last fall. They lost about four thousand dollars' worth of stuff, and the place was trashed. We didn't want that happening to us. And then, too, I'm on the road a lot. I travel for a copper fittings company, I'm their Midwest sales rep, so I'm on the road maybe four, five nights a week, and I didn't like the idea of my wife being there alone at night. Our neighborhood isn't what it used to be. Used to be, nobody even locked their doors at night."

Nathan moved forward and hooked his thumbs under his belt. "So in other words, you bought Max in a perfectly understandable effort to protect your wife and your property. From whom did you buy the dog?"

"From K-Nine Courage. It's a kennel in Mundelein, Illinois."

"A kennel specializing in guard dogs?"

"Yes, sir. They breed them and train them there, Dobermans and shepherds and Rottweilers. And they charge good and plenty, too, let me tell you."

"How much in this case, Mr. Jacobson? How much did you pay for Max?"

"Two thousand dollars. That sounds like a hell of a lot, but he came fully trained and guaranteed, and I figured it was worth it."

"Fully trained," Nathan said.

"Yes, sir. Max is trained for regular obedience commands, like come and sit and down, and he's also trained to attack on command and cease attacking on command."

"And what sort of attack is Max trained to do, can you tell the court?"

"Arm. To go for the arm."

All eyes in the room turned toward Mr. Phelps' bandaged left arm.

"I see," Nathan said. "And when you bought this dog, were you given instructions as to handling him?"

"Oh, sure. The trainer told my wife and me the command words and had us practice with Max there at the kennel."

"So at the time you purchased this dog, you had every reason to believe he was a well-trained and dependable guard dog, is that right?"

"Yes, sir. He came with a guarantee."

"For two thousand dollars."

"Yes, sir."

"Would you say, Mr. Jacobson, would you say that to a dog trained to guard his owner's property, a strange man coming in the back door with a large sack on his shoulders might be likely to appear to be a threat?"

"Yes, sir, I'd say so."

"Would you say that, in this dog's mind, he was merely doing his job, the job for which he had been highly trained?"

"Yes, sir."

"Would you say that in grabbing Mr. Phelps' arm your dog Max was in fact doing exactly what he had been trained to believe was right under the circumstances?"

"Yes. Sure."

"Were you at home at the time of the accident?"

"No, sir, I was out of town."

"Your wife was at home alone, is that right?"

"Yes, that's right."

"So your dog Max was entrusted with the protection of this woman, your wife, who was at home alone at the time that this apparently strange man, apparently threatening man—"

"Objection, Your Honor," from the other attorney.

Nathan said quickly, "Your Honor, I'm only trying to present the picture as it appeared to the dog."

"Overruled. Proceed."

David smiled. Chalk one up for Dad's side.

7

"Your dog was simply doing his job as he understood it. Would you say that was an accurate statement, Mr. Jacobson?"

"Yes."

Nathan said, "No more questions, Your Honor," and gave his client to the other attorney, who strode forward into battle.

"Now, Mr. Jacobson, did it never occur to you that owning an animal of this kind, trained to attack human beings, was a dangerous undertaking? Did it not occur to you that thousands of innocent people every year are attacked by supposedly well-trained guard dogs, and that by—"

"Objection," Nathan called. "Badgering the witness."

"Overruled, but watch it." The judge scowled at the plaintiff's attorney.

"And that by owning such a dog, Mr. Jacobson, you were running some risk that he might at some time attack an innocent person like Mr. Phelps here?"

"He came guaranteed," Jacobson insisted. He was a small man, dark and thin-haired and uncomfortable-looking in his position on the witness stand.

"And what precautions did you take, Mr. Jacobson, to ensure that the dog was under control at all times?"

"Well, we kept him on a chain in the yard when we weren't home, and in the house with us when we were home. He couldn't do his job as a watchdog if he was chained up all the time, could he?"

"And at the time of the attack, what safety precautions were in effect at that time, in regard to the dog?"

Mr. Jacobson frowned. "I don't understand the question."

8

"Was the dog under any kind of restraint on that afternoon?"

"He was in the house. With my wife."

"And what was your wife doing at the time Mr. Phelps came into the house?"

"She was talking on the phone."

"I see. Talking on the phone."

It sounded to David as though the attorney was trying to make it seem as though Mrs. Jacobson should have been hanging on to the dog every minute. A dumb approach, he decided. He wished it were a jury trial, so he could watch the faces of the jurors for their reactions to the other attorney's tactics and Nathan's. It was always more fun with a jury.

"No more questions." The attorney retired with a triumphant smile, as though he had just scored. Part of the act, David knew. Look victorious and people will think you must have been.

"May I approach the bench, Your Honor?" Nathan said, and David sat up straighter. This was the part he'd come to see. There was a whispered conference among the two attorneys and the judge, then the judge lifted his head and motioned toward the bailiff at the courtroom door.

The door swung open and a uniformed guard came in leading the dog. David pulled in his breath.

The dog was beautiful. He was as cleanly carved as a racehorse: long, narrow, elegant head, ears chopped off to form erect points, powerful chest, and legs made of long ridges of muscle and sinew. His tail was an almost invisible stub. The coat was short and hard and a brilliant polished black, set off by red-gold markings on his legs and beneath his tail. Twin tan spots showed over his eyes. A silver chain collar tightened around his throat as the guard shortened his grip on the lead.

The dog paced calmly down the center aisle, pausing for an instant while the guard maneuvered the swinging gate. The animal's elegant head turned; dark golden eyes met David's. Intelligence and dignity shone from their depths and stirred something in David that he had never expected to feel again.

2

"With Your Honor's permission," Nathan Purdy said, "I'd like to ask my son David to help me demonstrate my confidence in Max."

David tensed, startled. He hadn't even known his father was aware of his presence in the back of the courtroom. The judge nodded, and Nathan motioned to David to join him in the open space before the bench. David jammed his book into his back pocket and moved forward, awkward in his eagerness.

Nathan said, "Your Honor, I'd like David to go over to the dog, touch him, do whatever he wants to do with Max, with your permission. David, have you ever seen this dog before?"

"No, sir." David never called his father sir, but it seemed appropriate under these circumstances. He looked at his father, who nodded toward the dog still standing calmly beside the guard.

For a split second David thought about Mr. Phelps' bandaged arm and face. Then the dog met his gaze, and David was reassured. He approached the dog and reached to run his hand over the hard bones of Max's skull. The dog's eyes softened a fraction.

David relaxed and ran both hands down the dog's

neck, over his chest. "Hey, fella," he murmured. The dog's rear moved slightly in a wagging motion. David was delighted. Remembering suddenly that he was supposed to be putting on a show for the judge, David took the dog's leash from the guard and led Max around in a small circle, then he knelt and wrapped his arm around the sleek black body. The dog pressed against him, trembling so slightly that the tremors could only be felt, not seen.

"Thank you, David," Nathan said. "I submit to you, Your Honor, that if I had the slightest doubt about this animal's trustworthiness, nothing could have induced me to risk my only child's safety."

David knew his part was finished, but it was with reluctance that he handed Max's leash back to the guard. With one last stroke, the full length of the dog's back, David pushed through the low swinging gate and returned to his seat at the back of the room.

His palm still felt the hard slickness of the dog's coat; his chest still reverberated with the dog's trembling. An old hunger was awakening in David, a hunger he thought he had beaten down and buried under guilt. It had been six years now since Corky, and the guilt was still strong in David. But now, having touched Max, the need for a dog of his own began to swell again, to rise above the memory of Corky.

On the morning of David's seventh birthday his parents, winking at each other and smothering grins, had taken him for a ride in the car, destination a surprise. It had been a house with a sign in front advertising cocker spaniels and a pen in back full of round, woolly puppies.

All of the puppies were black, and at first they had

seemed identical to David, but one puppy worked more diligently than the others at attacking David's shoelaces and snatching at his pants cuffs. That puppy had gone home with them, on a towel in David's lap.

"She's going to be your responsibility," Nathan told David sternly. "I don't want to see you putting any of the work of that puppy off onto your mother. You know how busy she is. We'll help you get started, but Corky is your dog, and taking care of her will be your job."

How eagerly the small David had nodded and agreed; how proudly he had filled the water bowl and feed dish, and wiped up the puppy's puddles and taken her out into the back yard a dozen times a day for walks on the red plastic leash. Nathan and Natalie Purdy had nodded and smiled at the way David was learning responsibility.

As Corky grew up the puddles gradually disappeared and the trips to the back yard became fewer, but other problems emerged. The active, growing young dog, shut in the bathroom during the day while everyone was gone, began to claw madly at door and floor, trying to tunnel out. David's allowance disappeared into payments to his father for replacing the door and re-laying linoleum. Then the shower curtain was shredded, and the wicker wastebasket.

David began to notice wads of fur, like gray felt, on Corky's ears and legs and chest. A mop of curls grew atop the dog's head, and long beardlike wisps of hair sprouted from chin and muzzle. But the worst were the damp felted mats on the undersides of Corky's ears. They brushed against the wetness of her lips and collected slime and soured food. Gradually people began to wrinkle their noses when Corky climbed into their laps.

For Christmas David received a dog brush and comb. He brushed and brushed, he combed and combed, but neither the brush's soft bristles nor the thick plastic teeth of the comb could penetrate the felted mats, which by that time covered the little animal's entire body, even the top of her back. David knew that somehow this was all his fault, but he truly didn't understand how. In his confused shame he began avoiding Corky. He no longer let the pleading dog up onto his bed at night. He avoided touching her. Most of all he avoided meeting her eyes.

Finally the words were spoken from on high. Natalie made the pronouncement; Nathan didn't have the heart to. "David, if you can't take any better care of that dog, she's going to have to go to the pound. She's filthy, she stinks, you don't ever play with her anymore or pay any attention to her. We told you from the start she was going to be your responsibility, and you're just not living up to it."

David cried. He gave Corky a bath in the bathtub and tried once more with the brush and the comb. He even tried to cut out some of the mats with his mother's sewing scissors, but he accidentally nicked the edge of Corky's ear, and she snarled and snapped at him.

"Okay then, I don't care," he cried furiously. He slammed the door of his bedroom and tried to hide from the situation, but his mother came and got him and put him in the car with Corky.

"This is your responsibility," she said grimly, "and you're going to see it through to the end."

They drove the twenty miles north to Cedar Rapids

in silence, and pulled up beside the low brick County Humane Shelter.

"I'll go in with you," Natalie said, "but remember, honey, you have to learn responsibility, and sometimes the lessons hurt. I'm sorry it has to be this way."

The woman behind the counter looked down on the small boy leading a horrendously matted black cocker, and she didn't need to ask.

"I can't keep her anymore," David said, trying to control the trembling of his lips. "I didn't take good care of her, so could you find her a better home, please?"

"I'm sure we can," the woman said briskly, and turned to Natalie for details and payment of the fee. When the paperwork was done the woman came around the counter and picked up Corky in her arms. David opened his mouth to say good-bye, to say how sorry he was, but Corky was pleading with her eyes, struggling toward David, and he couldn't bear it. He turned and ran outside to huddle in the car, more miserable than he'd ever been in his life.

Several weeks later Natalie came across the folder containing Corky's registration papers, in a drawer she was cleaning. She called the Humane Shelter to see whether Corky's new owners would like to have the pedigree and registration slip. She was told that no one had come to adopt Corky within the allotted time limit, and that Corky had been put to sleep. Natalie, who believed in treating children like adults, told David.

It was months before he stopped having nightly dreams about Corky, not quite nightmares but dark, depressing dreams. Corky's eyes burned into his soul, huge spaniel eyes pleading for her life as she receded

15

from his grasp. And his mother loomed through the dreams, a tall, omnipotent shape whose voice came down to him saying, "You have to throw Corky away now. I'm tired of her."

In one dream, so terrible that flashes of it were still laced through David's dreams, his mother had said, "Tired of you. Tired of taking care of you. Going to take you to the shelter and leave you there." And she had been talking about David.

David's mind veered away from the memory of that dream, even when it was fresh, but for weeks after he first had it, he felt driven to make his bed the instant he was out of it, and to wash out the bathroom sink so there would be no white spatters of toothpaste spit for his mother to clean up.

If anyone had asked him, then or at any time, whether his mother loved him he would have said yes, of course, and said it without hesitation. His mother was a good person and good people loved their children. But somewhere deep within him a fear had been born. It made him put his hands in his pockets when they itched to touch a dog; it made him bury the urge within him for a dog of his own.

Until now.

The judge was pronouncing his decision. "I find the defendant, Joseph Jacobson, liable for damages amounting to"—he consulted his notes—"five thousand dollars medical expenses and mental anguish, in that he failed to sufficiently control a potentially dangerous animal.

"However, it is the court's belief that the dog, Max, was acting in a way consistent with his nature and training, and therefore there will be no further punishment of the dog nor will he be put to sleep at this time. Un-

16

der the one-bite law a dog is given the benefit of the doubt *once*, Mr. Jacobson. However, should this animal bite a second time he will be considered dangerous and will be put to sleep at the order of the court. Is that understood? After this, Mr. Jacobson, make certain that the dog is under complete control at all times, because a second incident such as this will be fatal for the dog and probably quite expensive for you."

"Yes, Your Honor."

The courtroom emptied quickly. David moved forward toward his father, Mr. Jacobson, and Max, still standing near their table. He bent to stroke the dog's head again, enjoying the feel of the marble-hard skull. Max leaned his head against David's leg, and once again the faint trembling buzzed through David. He wondered if the dog could possibly have understood that he'd been on trial for his life just now. David himself hadn't realized it until the judge had made his final statement.

Nathan glanced at David, then dropped an arm around his son's shoulders. "Thanks for your help, Dave. That was a spur-of-the-moment idea. You were great."

Mr. Jacobson snorted. "Fat lot of good it did. Five thousand, plus court costs, plus your fee. Hell, I'd have been better off if I'd never got the damn dog. Been better off letting my house be robbed."

David stared at the man. "Aren't you glad my dad got Max off, at least? Aren't you glad you don't have to have him put to sleep?"

"Glad?" The little man glared at David as though he were to blame. "Been a blessing, if you ask me. You think I want that dog back in my house after this?

17

You think I want to risk this happening again sometime? I'll tell you right now, I'm not taking that animal home with me. From here he goes straight to the vet or the pound, I don't care which, but he's a dead dog this minute as far as I'm concerned. Five thousand and court costs!"

He jerked the leash and started up the aisle, dragging the dog in his wake. David looked, pleaded, toward his father. Nathan met his gaze but didn't understand the message.

"I want him," David breathed.

"You? Want that dog? Are you nuts?"

"Please, Dad. You defended him. You must have believed in him. Please, Dad, he's going to be put down if we don't take him. You heard Mr. Jacobson."

"I defended him because it was my job to. I trusted him with you because he wasn't on his home turf so I knew he wouldn't be likely to be aggressive, he wouldn't be defending his own territory. That doesn't mean I want a dog like that in my home."

"Can we just try, Dad? Just try, just for a few days, see how it goes?"

"But why, all of a sudden?" Nathan frowned, trying to understand. "You've never said a word all these years about wanting a dog. Not since . . ."

Not since Corky. The thought hung in the air between them.

Nathan said, "Is that what this is about? Corky? Are you trying to . . . make up for something?"

"I don't know." David shrugged, then moved toward the door, urging his father along with body English. "Hurry, Dad, catch him before he gets away. Please. It's important to me."

18

Nathan's face puckered in concerned thought. Finally he shrugged. David turned and ran.

He caught up with Mr. Jacobson in the parking lot, just as Max was leaping into the back seat of the man's car.

"Mr. Jacobson. Wait." David came up panting. "My dad said I could have Max, if that's okay with you."

"Have him?" The man seemed nonplussed.

"Well, you said you didn't want him. You said you were going to have him put to sleep. Wouldn't you rather give him to me? He'll have a good home, I promise."

"You actually want this dog, after what he just cost me in there?"

David smiled.

"Well, I think you're nuttier than a fruitcake, kid, and your dad is, too, for going along with it. But . . . good luck." With that he motioned the dog out of the car and handed David the leash. "Good luck," he said again. "You'll need it."

The car pulled away as Nathan approached. David stood on the asphalt of the parking lot, looking down at the dog beside him and thinking, *What have I let myself in for?*

Leaving his bike to be retrieved later, David rode home beside his father, the dog stretched across the back seat.

Darkly Nathan muttered, "Your mother is going to love this."

3

Although the state university, where Natalie Purdy taught clinical psychology, was on its spring break, Natalie was busier than usual that week, organizing a graduate seminar on transactional analysis. It always seemed to David that his mother worked frantically at filling up her vacation time with extra projects, so that her life never had any downtime in it.

Natalie was fifty-one that spring, and her race toward accomplishments seemed to be speeding up, as though she were seeing a time limit. Once when David was nine he had remarked on the fact that his parents were older than his friends' parents. Natalie had told him, yes, his arrival had been an unplanned event in their lives and that, although they were happy to have him, they had decided before he was born that they intended to go on with their own lives as fully as possible in spite of parenthood. David hadn't answered, but someplace deep inside he still bore the scars of that conversation.

Still, at times like this, David was glad that his mother's life was not focused on him. He had no serious fears about her saying a flat no to Max, with Dad on his side.

20

David spent the afternoon with the dog, walking him around the house and yard, showing him his territory. It was a roomy old frame house on the north edge of Iowa City, tall and angular and white and overgrown with lilacs and spruce trees. It had begun as a farmhouse, but the barns and fields were gone now, swallowed up in the building boom of the forties and fifties. Pastel ranch houses covered the hills and closed in around the Purdys' old farmhouse, making it seem out of place although it had seniority by eighty years.

The rooms were square and high-ceilinged, with polished bare floors that Natalie had never gotten around to softening with rugs. The furniture was a haphazard collection of good pieces and junk, but it hardly mattered because every surface was covered with books, papers, litter. It could have been a warm and comfortable house, but it just missed. No one cared enough about it to create areas of comfort within it.

David and Max spent most of the afternoon in David's room, where he felt confident enough to unsnap the dog's leash and let him roam and sniff as he pleased. The dog seemed to be cataloging scents, as though he knew this place and this person were his new assignment. David lay across his bed watching the dog and wondering whether he should be afraid of Max. He wasn't, yet, but the image of Mr. Phelps and his bandages was not far beneath his surface thoughts, and sometimes he stared at Max's long powerful jaws. . . .

Still, the dog seemed to like David. He finished his circling tours and leaped up onto the bed to stretch, full length, beside David. Lying that way, they were the same length. David stroked the hard black coat, felt the rocklike muscles of the dog's neck. Max lay head up and

21

alert at first, but gradually under the even strokes of David's hand, the chopped-off ears relaxed and the head lowered to lie on the sinewy forelegs. The eyes didn't close, but they softened.

What have I got myself into? David thought over and over. All these years he'd lived under the guilt of failing in his responsibility to Corky, and that had been just a matter of grooming. This now, this was so much bigger. So much worse. This was a dog that could conceivably kill a person. And David had opened his mouth in a hurried moment and taken on the responsibility that even grown men hadn't wanted. Not even the man who paid two thousand dollars for this dog. The thought chilled David in the pit of his stomach.

Natalie got home just after Nathan, at suppertime. She was a short, stocky woman whose gray-streaked hair was pulled back in a ponytail. She wore slacks and a poncho. As she moved about the kitchen throwing together a salad for their supper, she muttered to herself, carrying on an imaginary argument with her department head.

She looked up as David led Max into the kitchen, looked again more closely at the dog, but didn't lose her rhythm chopping celery.

"Hi, hon, where'd that beast come from?"

"A guy gave him to me. Can I keep him?"

"What guy?"

Nathan lumbered in from the living room, the evening paper between his fingers. "Better tell her the truth, the whole truth, Dave. Hi, lover-lump." He kissed the top of Natalie's head. She bent in for the kiss but went on chopping.

22

"What whole truth? What have you guys been up to?"

David told her.

She widened her eyes and looked harder at Max, who lowered his muscular rump to the floor and sat close beside David's leg. "This is the dog you were defending in that attack case? You gave him to your son for a pet? Wonderful."

"It was David's idea," Nathan said. "I'm not crazy about it, but it seemed important to Dave, and I said we'd try it for a day or two anyhow, subject to your approval of course, and just see how it went. I also said, any sign of trouble and he goes to dog heaven."

Natalie puffed her cheeks out and blew a long sigh that lifted a strand of hair from her forehead. She cocked a look at Max, and he moved his stub of a tail across the floor. Natalie shrugged and began dumping chopped ingredients into a big wooden salad bowl. "Well, he doesn't look too ferocious. Nate, there's a loaf of French bread in there. Would you stick it in the oven? Bread and salad be enough for you guys, or do you want some of that spinach soufflé? This enough?"

"Can I keep him then?" David asked as he took his place at the refectory table in a jungle of hanging plants at the far end of the kitchen.

"Oh, I suppose, for now anyway," Natalie said as she fished bottles of dressing out of the refrigerator. "We'll see how he behaves."

"He's very well trained," David said. "Max, down." The dog stretched out on the floor beside David's feet.

For an instant David wasn't sure whether he was glad about his mother's verdict or not. *Well, I'm in this for sure now,* he told himself. He was glad supper was light tonight; his stomach would have clenched against a bigger meal.

The next morning, as soon as he had the house to himself, David called the nearest veterinarian and asked the receptionist if there was anyone in that part of town who knew about training dogs. Try Sally Borcharding, the receptionist suggested, Sal-Bar Kennel out on Highway One, and she gave him the phone number.

It rang five times before a voice barked, "Sal-Bar Kennels."

"Is this Mrs. Borcharding?"

"Speaking. What can I do for you?" The voice sounded harsh but not unfriendly, David decided.

"Um, my name is David Purdy, and I just got this dog, he's a Doberman pinscher and he's been trained for guard dog work, see, and he bit a guy, and now I've got him and I was wondering if there's anything you can suggest for training him, I mean, more for like untraining him. . . ."

David wasn't sure what he was asking, but the woman seemed to understand.

"You want to deprogram him so he doesn't get in trouble again, right?"

"Yeah." David sighed with relief.

"Well," the woman snorted, "lots of luck."

"Do you mean there isn't anything I can do? He seems like a really nice dog. I love him already," David pleaded.

"You sound like a kid. How old are you?"

"Thirteen."

"And your folks let you have this attack-trained Doberman, huh?"

David was silent, wounded.

The woman sighed. "Okay, listen, I don't think there's a whole lot I can tell you, but if you feel like stopping by here sometime I'll take a look at your dog, tell you what I think, anyhow. He doesn't have any diseases, does he?"

"No," David bristled. "He's very healthy."

"No offense, kid. I got thousands of dollars worth of show dogs here in my kennel. You can understand why I'm a little cautious of visiting dogs, with all this parvo and kennel cough going around and who knows what all else."

"Can I come today?"

"Sure, why not. Not till after lunch, though. I got two litters of pups to clean up after. I won't be out from under morning chores till then. You come around one. Half a mile north of the city limits sign on Highway One, east side of the road, big blue house, sign out in front. You can't miss it."

David made peanut butter sandwiches and packed them, with two apples and a small can of V-8, in his backpack book bag and started the hike toward downtown and his abandoned bike. Max paced happily beside him.

"I should have got a ride with Dad this morning, dumb me," he said, but he didn't really mind the walk. Max was good company. He'd forgotten how nice it felt to go walking with a dog, and Max was especially good at it. He stayed close to David's left hip, unlike Corky, who had darted from side to side and dragged constantly against the leash. David's hand rode companionably on the dog's back, and together they noticed trees budding and tulips blooming.

As they neared the downtown area and sidewalk traffic thickened, David saw with some pleasure that people looked at Max with admiration or respect and circled out of the dog's reach. Still Max behaved perfectly. David began to relax about him.

In the courthouse parking lot David retrieved his bike and, with some uneasiness about how this was going to work, got on and began pedaling one-handed, Max's leash in the other hand. At first the dog looked warily at the nearness of wheels and pedals, but within the first block they had hit their stride and were moving smoothly, dog and bike in balance.

At a small park in a residential area they stopped for lunch on the grass, with the crusts going to Max. An elderly man walked past with a miniature schnauzer in a red felt coat. Max lifted his head and muttered deep in his throat. David tensed.

"No, Max. No growling." He spoke in a low hard voice, and jerked lightly on Max's collar. The growling ceased, but Max followed the small dog with hot eyes.

They continued out the street that was also Highway One, north through shady neighborhoods, up and down steep hills, and finally into the beginning of open fields. Here they rode on the graveled shoulder of the narrow highway, to keep Max safe from passing traffic. It was hard pumping, and David's legs ached with weariness by the time he saw the blue house and the dog-shaped sign at the lane entrance. "Sal-Bar Golden Retrievers, champion stud service, puppies usually available."

David leaned his bike against a tree and shortened

his hold on Max's leash. The dog was tense and alert now, straining toward the scents of the dogs behind the house.

No one answered his knock at the side door, but as he was turning to look for another door, a woman appeared around the corner of the house. She was big and broad-shouldered within a faded flannel shirt and jeans. About the age of his mother, David guessed. Pale hair cropped short, weathered skin, cigarette dangling from the corner of her mouth.

"Are you Mrs. . . . ?" David couldn't remember her name.

"Borcharding, but call me Sally. You're the kid with the attack dog. Obviously." She looked down at Max with a professional stare. "This is him, huh? What's his name?"

"Max."

"Hey, Max." She ran her hands over the dog.

"What do you think of him?" David said finally.

The woman shrugged and dragged on her cigarette. "Well, he's no show dog, that's for sure. Too skully, too straight in the shoulders, not enough tan in his markings. But what the hell, you didn't get him for show, so that's not important. Here, let's put him in this empty run for now, and I'll show you my critters, and then we can talk."

She led the way to a red barn with a row of chain link runs along one side. The end run was unoccupied, and she ushered Max into it and snapped his leash onto the wire of the gate. David relaxed then, glad to have his hands free from the responsibility of controlling Max.

A gravel path bordered the row of runs. Sally led the way, pausing before each run to introduce the dogs within. They were all golden retrievers, large, woolly dogs shading from pale sandy cream to a rich red gold, all with broad smiling heads and warm dark eyes. David reached through the wire with his fingers, and the dogs sniffed, licked, positioned themselves for scratching and petting.

"These two in here are both retired champions, on brood bitch duty now. That's Champion Sal-Bar's Flirt, CD, and that's her litter sister, Champion Sal-Bar's Flair, CDX. She's my darlin', aren't you, Flairy? Dam of nine finished champions and four more major-pointed and coming along."

David nodded and looked as though he knew what she was talking about. It all sounded impressive, and he was indeed impressed. "What do the letters stand for, CD? Is that what you said?"

"Those are obedience titles. Companion Dog, Companion Dog Excellent. My stud dog's a UDT and OTCH. That's Utility Dog, Tracking, and Obedience Trial Champion. And Bench Champion, too. That's about all the honors you can get on one dog except for field champion, and I don't get into that. That's him in that last run. There's my Bear." She lifted her voice and the dog in the end run leaped against the wire, joyous at her approach. "That's my foundation sire there, Sal-Bar's Bruin, plus all his titles. Friends call him Bear, though, don't they, you old fool?"

Sally opened the gate and the dog bounded out to fling himself against her, then against David, then back to Sally. "Poor thing never gets any attention, do you?" she crooned.

The dog was a bright new-penny gold with pale cream feathering on his legs and tail, and just a suggestion of gray in his muzzle. He romped across the lawn, snatched the remains of an old shoe, and brought it to David.

"You're supposed to throw it," Sally said.

David threw; the dog bounded after it, tossing it in the air before he brought it back to David.

"That's enough," Sally said. "He'll keep fetching as long as you keep throwing, and that could go on all day. Come on in the house where we can sit in comfort. You can leave your dog there where he is, for now. Let's get us something to drink and see if we can come up with anything useful about deprogramming attack dogs."

Bear led the way to the house, optimistic that he would be invited in. He was.

4

They settled in the denlike living room, in deep chairs shaggy with dog hair. David had a cold can of 7-Up, Sally a can of Coors. The dog, Bear, lay on his back in the center of the room, playing idiotically with a knotted sock held between forepaws.

The room was paneled in knotty pine; the walls were covered with shelves that held forests of dog show trophies, most of them in need of dusting. There were photographs, too, of golden retrievers being held in show pose with Sally towering over them and smiling judges holding rosettes and silver bowls.

"Wow," David said in succinct comment.

"Yeah, wow. Well, it represents a lifetime of hauling to shows every weekend. You have to accumulate a little hardware along the way when you're that nuts."

"Does your husband go, too?"

Sally barked out a harsh laugh. "Old Barney? He did, he used to, first ten or twelve years we were married. Then one day he says to me, he says, 'Sal, I've had it with these damn dogs. Either the dogs go or I go.' His exact words."

David was mildly startled. He wasn't used to talking about marital problems with strange adults. "What did you say?" he asked finally, since she seemed to be waiting for him to deliver the straight line.

"Why, I said, 'There's the door, but leave me the station wagon.' I needed it for my dog show trips." She laughed a deep rich laugh, and David grinned.

"Oh, well"—Sally slapped her leg—"he wasn't all that great a loss. He sure was no competition for a good Golden. But you didn't come out here to talk about my dogs, you came to talk about yours. Hmm. Do you know what kind of training he had before you got him? Was it Schutzhund or guard or attack or what? Does he know basic obedience? Will he heel and sit and all that?"

"I think so," David said, frowning. "I mean, he sits when I tell him to. I don't know about the rest of what you said."

Sally slid deeper in her chair, propped her booted feet on a pile of dog magazines on the hassock, and frowned down at the beer can on her stomach.

"Boy, I don't know. This is out of my field, you understand. I've done all levels of obedience work and put a few tracking titles on a few dogs, but I never wanted anything to do with any kind of guard or attack training."

"Why was that?" David tried to settle back as casually as she did.

"Hate it. Hate the whole idea of it. Well, of course, you wouldn't likely do it with a breed like Goldens, anyway. It's not in their nature. You see, you got your groups. Your breeds all fall into seven groups: sporting, hound, working, terrier, toy, nonsporting, and herding. And each one of these groups is designed for special purposes, or do you already know all this stuff?"

31

David shook his head.

"Okay then. Goldens are in the sporting group, all your retrievers and pointers and setters and spaniels, and like that. They've got bird hunting instincts bred into them, and along with that, they've got peaceable natures, toward people and toward other dogs."

David nodded. "What about Dobermans, then?"

"Well now, there you're getting into your working group, and you've got a high degree of desire to please, but you've also got a strong streak of territorial instinct—in some of the breeds anyway. A dog like a Doberman, he knows his territory, be it his house, car, whatever, and woe betide anybody that dog doesn't like, who dares to trespass on that dog's turf.

"Your Doberman is engineered to be a fighting animal. You look at him and you'll see there's not a wrinkle of loose skin anywhere on that dog. You know why? So his opponents can't get a hold on him in a fight. His ears are cropped so they won't get torn in a fight. He's about as quick and agile and powerful as any dog going, and he's designed sleek like that on purpose. Most dogs attack you and you can get a grip of some loose flesh around the neck area to hold them off. Bear, come here. See? Here. I could get a fistful of pelt right there and hold him away from me." She wrestled lovingly with the dog, pushed him away, fended him off when he bounced back for more play.

"But not on a Doberman," Sally went on, more soberly. "Now that's not necessarily bad. Hell, they're beautiful dogs. I admire them. I wouldn't take one as a gift, but then I can't see any reason for anyone wanting any dog that's not a Golden, and that's my blind spot." She laughed.

"Still," she said, "the trouble these days isn't so much with the breed as it is with the breeders and trainers and opportunists." She paused for a long drink.

"Opportunists? Like what?" David asked.

She leveled a look at him. "Like people who mass produce these dogs, mainly Dobes and shepherds and Rottweilers, with no concern for the dogs' mental and physical health, give them the worst kind of so-called training, and then peddle them for big bucks to jerks who don't know what they're getting into. Oh, it's a full-blown racket, Dave. You can take my word on that."

He sat forward. "What do you mean about the worst kind of training?"

She drained her can and crumpled it and tossed it toward a wastebasket in the corner. Bear retrieved it.

"I mean the so-called attack training that a lot of these dogs get. Right now everybody is all hot to get a watchdog. Get a guard dog. It's stupid, but what can you say to people? Lots of guys have this macho thing where they just love owning a dog everybody else is afraid of. That's part of it. And lots of people are genuinely worried about their safety. Lord knows the rape statistics in Iowa City this last year are darn near enough to make anyone think about guard dogs."

"So then, what's wrong with people buying guard dogs?"

"What's wrong is that so many of these dogs aren't trained to the point of being safe." Sally sat forward earnestly. "See, the average normal dog has a strong instinct in him that forbids him ever to bite a human being. The vast majority of dogs never bite, or if they do it's a controlled bite, a light snap maybe when you're

33

combing them and you pull too hard, something like that."

David remembered Corky.

"But for the most part, a dog will not bite a human being, and that's because they accept us as dominant over them. Dogs are pack animals, with the same pack instincts as wolves, and in a wolf pack there is the alpha wolf, the leader. Every other wolf in that pack knows better than to challenge the alpha wolf and they just don't do it. Well, in domesticated dogs, it's the same thing. A dog accepts his person as the alpha wolf in their two-animal pack, and he never challenges."

David nodded, fascinated.

"Well, then you give a dog this so-called attack training, and what it amounts to is brainwashing the dog, something like soldiers losing their natural instinct against killing another human being. More often than not the dog is teased or hurt to make it furious, and then praised when it attacks a human. You do that often enough, especially with a dog with a strong aggressive nature to begin with, like your Dobes and Rotts, and you've got a problem."

David was silent. A sick sort of churning began in his stomach, hearing her words and thinking about Max.

"So what do you think I should do then, about Max? Should I let them go ahead and put him down, do you think?"

Sally's broad face softened. "How should I know? Listen, don't take me too seriously. Like I said before, I really can't see beyond my own breed. Your dog may never be a problem. The world is full of perfectly nice Dobes who never bite."

"He already did," David said in a low voice. "That's

how I got him. He attacked a delivery man who came in his house and ripped the guy's arm up pretty badly. My dad was the defense lawyer in the case. The judge said it really wasn't the dog's fault under the circumstances, but Max's owner didn't want him back after that. It cost him five thousand dollars in damages, plus court costs and my dad's fee. So he was going to have Max put down, and I took him instead."

"Ah."

They sat for a long time without talking. Bear brought the knotted sock to David and clawed at his arm until David played tug-of-war with him, but the boy's mind was outside with Max.

Slapping her knees, Sally rose suddenly. "Let's go out and have another look at this beast. Bear, you stay in here. Stay. And that means off the kitchen table, you hear me?"

They went outside, retrieved Max from his run, and walked with him to an area behind the kennel-barn, where a large square space was roped off in a semblance of a dog show ring. Along one side stood white painted jumps.

Sally took Max's lead and walked into the ring. "Let me just see what he knows, okay? Max, *heel*." She started walking and Max trotted close to her side. She stopped, Max stopped and slowly sat.

"Stay," she barked, motioning with the flat of her hand. She walked away and Max stayed where he sat.

She returned, walking around behind the dog. "Down," she barked, and Max lowered himself to the ground. Then she walked him to the far side of the ring, left him on the sit-stay command, and crossed the ring. She turned and faced him and yelled, "Max, *come.*"

He lay down, ears flattened.

"Come," she bellowed again, and this time he came toward her, slinking low, and halted several feet in front of her. "Come," she commanded again. He lowered himself and crept in closer.

"Heel." She made a motion with her left arm and the dog crept in a circle to return to her left side, in heel position, but his head was low and his eyes hostile.

Sally bent and picked up the dragging leash and brought the dog back to David. She shook her head and pulled her mouth to one side.

"I don't know," she said, handing over the leash. "He's been obedience trained, that's obvious. So whoever trained him didn't just give him a crash course in aggression, like a lot of them do. At least he's had some groundwork in the basics, so possibly the trainer wasn't a complete rip-off artist. But on the other hand, I don't much like the way he responded on that come-on-recall exercise. He looked like he wanted to rip my throat out."

"He looked scared of you," David said, but without much optimism.

"Yeah, I know. He acted like he'd been handled pretty rough in the training process. Maybe the guy used spiked collars or electric collars or some such. I don't know what to tell you, kid." She sighed again.

David started moving toward his bike, wanting to be away from here, wanting not to have to hear any more.

Sally walked with him. "I suppose you've fallen in love with the dog," she said glumly.

David nodded and stroked Max's head.

36

"Well"—Sally shrugged and smiled—"we don't always love wisely, do we? Look at the jerk I married. I guess my best advice to you, if you want to try to de-program this dog, would be, let's see. A couple of things. Give him lots of exercise and don't stick him out on a chain somewhere. Dogs that are chained seem to get meaner than blazes, probably because they have such a small territory that they get over-possessive of it. If you've got a fenced yard, great. If not, maybe you can build him a fenced run so he can work off his nervous energy. Go running with him, anything. But at the same time, don't let him run loose. Keep him under control at all times. Don't trust him. And if I were you I wouldn't try to do any training of any kind with him. Not for now, anyway. Let him relax, let him cool down, give him as much exercise as you possibly can, and don't ever trust him completely, at least not till he's proved he's trustworthy."

David nodded and mounted his bike. "Thanks for all your time and trouble. I really appreciate it."

"My pleasure. Come out again if you feel like it. Any time. I like kids. I like kids who love dogs. Oh, one other thing," she said as he began to pedal away, "one other thing, and this is important. Never, never let that dog get the better of you. If he growls at you and you back off from him, just once, that's going to prove to him that *he* is the alpha wolf between the two of you. If that happens, kid, you've had it. You'll never be able to discipline him after that."

Wide-eyed, David nodded.

"Enjoyed your visit," Sally called brightly. "Come again."

5

When David asked his parents about the possibility of fencing in the back yard for Max, they discussed it and decided no. Nathan called the lumberyard and priced dog-tight fencing high enough to stop a Doberman, did some figuring on his scratch pad, and declared that seven hundred dollars was way more than they could justify for a dog who was in the family only on probation in the first place.

"Then how about just a fenced run, maybe along the side of the garage?" David asked. Nathan refigured and pronounced the new verdict, more like a hundred dollars, and if David wanted to help pay for it he would help build it.

"But let's wait awhile," Nathan urged. "I'm still not anywhere near convinced that this dog is going to be a permanent member of the household. Two days of good behavior is not really much of a test, is it?"

"But Sally said it was important to give him a place to work off his energy," David insisted, and so the next Saturday the lumberyard delivered thirty feet of five-foot-high chain link, a gate, and six stout timbers. The bill came to one hundred forty dollars, fifty dollars more than David had in his savings account. Nathan chipped in the balance.

As the two of them began measuring and digging the post holes, Max lay tied to a tree, watching them. David had taken him for a long run early that morning, so he was comfortably stretched and tired. David was tired, too. Not comfortably. He had a forlorn hope that all this dog running might burn some fat off of his mid-section, but so far, after five days, all it had done was prove to him how out of shape he was. He puffed, now, digging the hole for the corner post.

"Now when we get this done," Nathan said, grunting as he eased the timber down into its hole, "I don't want you sticking Max out here and forgetting about him. That's all too easy to do, with an outdoor dog."

"No, I know. I still want him in the house with me whenever I'm home. This is just for a safe place to put him while I'm in school. And I'll still take him for a couple of long runs every day."

"Stout fellow." Nathan grinned.

It took all of Saturday to get the posts set, the wire fastened securely around them, and the gate hung. David led Max into the run and watched him through the wire, admiring the picture. The run was twenty feet long by five feet wide, and used the end wall of the garage as one of its long sides. It was shaded by the garage and a large maple tree, and carpeted with grass. A pleasant place for a dog to live, David thought with deep satisfaction. And safe. As the thought flashed through his mind, David avoided examining it too closely. Safe *for* Max . . . safe *from* him?

There was a streak of realism in David's nature that

made him acknowledge unpleasant facts, such as his own fear of pain, and the trickling, prickling fear he felt when he looked at Max's powerful body and long curving eyeteeth, and envisioned them ripping into his flesh.

In these few days since Max had become the center of his life, David had not been threatened, but he knew the testing time would come, and the knowledge was cold and heavy in his stomach.

After supper that night Nathan yawned and scratched his chest and challenged David to a game of eight ball. On ticking toenails Max followed them down the basement stairs and prowled the dark places behind the furnace while David and Nathan chose their cues and did a ritual chalking.

Father and son were uniformly uncoordinated at the game. They sprawled over the table making clumsy stabs that sometimes missed even the cue ball.

"Okay, now watch this," Nathan said. "Three ball in the corner pocket. Now watch, this is going to be beautiful."

"When cows fly," David scoffed.

"When cows fly, don't look up." Nathan made his shot; the three ball missed the corner pocket by several inches.

David whooped and moved around the table to line up his shot. "How much did we say we were playing for? Five thousand dollars?"

"How about . . . nineteen cents?"

"Sounds like a nice round number. Okay now, here goes. Three ball in the corner pocket."

The shot was a success.

"Oh well, of course," Nathan snorted. "I got it up to the very brink for you. Any fool could have—"

"David," Natalie called from above, "your dog is on the davenport."

⌐"Better get him off," Nathan warned.

The davenport was the one sacrosanct piece of furniture in the house. It was an antique, of pale cream, woolly fabric, crewel-embroidered, and it had belonged to Natalie's mother, who had died a few months before. David lay down his cue and bounded up the stairs.

Natalie was standing in the middle of the living room, staring down at Max, who lay full length on the davenport, with the remains of a very-long-dead mouse between his forelegs. There had been traps set and forgotten, behind the furnace. Max lowered his head and glared at Natalie and at David.

"I tried to get him off," Natalie said, "but he growled at me. He's your dog. You get him off there. And the mouse."

For an instant David stood, just looking. He dreaded this. He dreaded Max's threatening him because he knew that he had to master him. Sally had said so, strongly, and David knew it was true. If Max felt himself to be dominant over David, if the dog knew he could frighten David, then there was no hope. Max would grow worse with every confrontation, and someday he would attack.

Now or never.

He stepped closer and made his voice hard. "Max, down! Get off there."

The dog lowered his head another fraction over the

41

mouse corpse. His eyes glittered, his throat rumbled a warning.

David wanted to run away from all of this. He forced himself a step closer and pointed toward the floor. "Bad Max. Bad dog. Get off of there right now."

The snakelike head lowered again, the black lips drew back in a hideous grin that showed wet white teeth.

"David," Natalie warned, "maybe you'd better call your father."

"I have to do this. He's my dog."

David knew he had to do something quickly. Already a light of triumph seemed to glow in the dog's eyes. He turned and ran to the kitchen, where Max's leash hung by the door. With the leash in his hand he went back to the dog and quickly, before he had time to think and lose his nerve, he reached forward and snapped the leash on to Max's choke chain collar.

A feeling of control washed through him and he jerked Max hard toward him. "Get down off of there," he commanded.

The dog slipped to the floor and moved toward David with softened eyes and apologetic tail. David stroked his head with an unsteady hand. "That's better. Now you know who's boss, don't you?"

"Here. The mouse." Natalie handed him a Kleenex.

"Yuck," David said as he wrapped the Kleenex around the corpse and put it in the garbage. Nathan came up the stairs looking concerned.

"What's going on up here? Aren't you going to finish our game?"

"I don't feel like it. I'm going to take Max for a run."

"You forfeit the nineteen cents."

42

"Put it on my bill."

Through the blue-aired twilight David and Max ran, jogged, ran, walked, circled several blocks and came to rest finally on their own back steps when it grew too dark to see. Night insects sang in harsh overlapping choruses; lightning bugs flashed against the dark line of the trees at the end of the yard.

David thought about summer nights when he was small, when he had run after the lightning bugs and caught them in a drinking glass with his hand pressed hard over its top.

"I caught thirty-eleven lightning bugs, so pay me," he would demand of his father or his mother, and they would say, "You get thirty-eleven sweet hugs and kisses, then." They would grab at him and he'd squirm away, wrinkling his face.

"I don't want sweet hugs and kisses. You have to pay me."

"What do you want money for?"

"For a puppy."

And then there had been Corky, and after that he was too grown-up to sell lightning bugs for sweet hugs and kisses. And he didn't want a puppy anymore.

He leaned back against the steps and against Max, who lay panting lightly on the top step. Twisting, he looked down at the dog and ran his hand slowly over Max's ribs again and again, feeling the shallow valleys between them, feeling the short hard coat that became bare skin behind the dog's elbow.

There was a darkness inside David that was separate from his mixed feelings about Max. It centered around his mother. In the night stillness David's orderly mind worked at that dark area, like fingers picking at a knotted string.

He was old enough now to know that his small-boy fears of his mother abandoning him, as she had made him abandon Corky, were unrealistic. Still, there had been so many times when she had hurt him or failed him in small ways; school open houses that she promised to come to, to see his drawings or test papers on display, but at the last minute a student would call and need her.

He was an unplanned intrusion in his parents' life. He knew that. He had been told. And no amount of being good ever seemed to be quite enough.

And now this, tonight. The dark mood mushroomed under David's probing. Tonight. Tonight she had stood there while he was being threatened by a dangerous animal, and *not done anything*. How much could she care about him, honestly, if she could just stand there like that? If she could go on letting him keep Max, knowing he might be dangerous?

David shook his head at his own illogic. He wanted to keep Max. He needed to succeed with Max. He would fight his parents any way he could to be allowed to keep the dog.

And yet . . .

And yet he resented them, her, he resented *her* for letting him.

"He's okay, he's just sitting on the back steps. I can see his foot." Nathan stood close to the bedroom window so he could see straight down to the small back porch below. He wore only his shorts, wild red and orange pinwheel-design boxer shorts. He took secret delight in

44

wearing the most garish shorts he could buy, under the enforced blandness of his lawyer suits. His bare feet were huge and white, with curved yellow nails.

"I wish you'd trim those toenails," Natalie said. "You tear holes in your socks." She was sitting up in bed with a magazine across her knees, but she hadn't been able to concentrate enough to read it.

She was still shaken over the dog business. She looked at her magazine but saw the Doberman's lowered head, bared fangs. She saw her son's arms and throat, exposed, vulnerable.

"Nate, we've got to do something about that dog. We're all scared of him, even David. You should have seen his face tonight trying to get that beast off the davenport. He was scared stiff, and I don't blame him. Toenails," she said as Nathan started to climb in beside her.

He went obediently into the adjoining bathroom and began making loud snapping noises with the toenail cutter.

"I don't know," he said. "I'm kicking myself for letting him have the dog in the first place. I know that was mistake number one. But I don't feel as though it would be right to go back on it now, for no good reason. I mean, he did handle the dog, honey. He mastered him and made him mind, and the dog didn't actually do anything but growl and try to bully him. Lots of dogs do that."

"Sure. Little dogs. This is different and you know it. I'm afraid he's going to get hurt, Nate."

Nathan turned out the lights and rolled in beside her to wrap her in his night-talking hug. Their bodies settled comfortably together.

He said, "I think we should give it a while, honey. David needs this experience."

"He needs to be snarled at by a man-eating monster?"

Nathan chuckled softly and bumped her to him in a hug. "No, what I think is going on here is that he's still feeling some kind of guilt about Corky, and now with this dog he can be, you know, saving a life."

"You mean because Corky was put to sleep? He doesn't feel guilty about that, does he? Surely he wouldn't . . ."

Nathan's head nodded against hers. "I believe he does. Well, look at it from his viewpoint. He didn't take care of Corky, so Corky died."

"That's not the way it was."

"Well, that's probably the way it seemed to him. And in a way, it *was* the way it was."

"Yes, but that wasn't really his fault. None of us knew beans about taking care of a dog. We had no idea how to handle that matted-coat situation."

"I know," Nathan soothed.

"What I kick myself about," she went on, "is telling him the dog was put to sleep. I should have had better sense than that. I'm supposed to be a psychologist, for heaven's sake."

"Psychologists make mistakes with their kids. Dentists' kids get cavities, doctors' kids get measles."

"I know," she sighed, turning away from him, "but I planned to be such a perfect mother. Remember when I was pregnant, how we used to lie awake nights talking about how we were going to raise our child absolutely perfectly?"

Nathan chuckled. "I remember. We both said we'd

probably goof every now and then, but neither of us really believed it."

She stretched and thrashed her legs through the sheets. "Well, I said it then and I still believe it; the best mothers are the ones who don't make slaves of themselves for their children, and keep a life for themselves so they don't get overly dependent on their children for all their satisfactions in life."

"I'm not arguing," Nathan said placidly.

"Well, give me an opinion, counselor. Do I carry it too far?"

"How should I know," he chuckled. "I have exactly as much parenting experience as you do."

She made a small squeak of exasperation and rolled close to him again. He drew her in and stroked her hair. "It ain't easy, kiddo, but it's worth it."

She mumbled into his neck.

6

After that night Max made no further attempt to challenge David's authority. When David had to remove a tennis shoe from the dog's mouth, Max lowered his head and stiffened, but neither growled nor bared his teeth as the shoe was pulled away.

The dog seemed willing, even glad, to acknowledge David as the alpha wolf in their two-animal pack. From that point on, he showed a marked affection for the boy. He wagged his stub tail at David's approach and pulled his lips back in what appeared to be a sort of grin. His hard head pressed against David's thigh when they walked together, and during meals Max lay with his chin and one paw across David's toe, as though holding the boy in place.

They ran easily together, Max matching his pace with David's. There were no sidewalks in this block, so they ran along the edge of the street, waving when the occasional car passed them. Max behaved perfectly except for barking at, and trying to chase, two eight-year-old girls as they pedaled past on their bikes one evening. One of them, Joyce Bates, stuck her tongue out at Max when she was safely past, and waved her foot at him in a kicking motion.

"Don't tease him," David yelled. "This is an attack dog."

"Oh, yeah? I bet." She glared at David and pedaled faster, pulling her handlebars from side to side as she caught up with her friend and disappeared around a corner.

For the first time David felt a tiny thrill at being the master of an animal other people feared and respected, even though Joyce's way of showing it was unpleasant. He could begin to understand a little why men bought attack dogs.

He slowed to a walk to ease the stitch in his side, and turned toward home. While his hand was at his side, he pinched the roll of excess David above his belt and wondered if it might be getting a little smaller after all. He looked down at Max, at the sleek hardness of the animal, and suddenly understood another facet of the attraction he had felt when he first saw Max in the courtroom five days ago. Max was what David wished to be.

The next day David talked down his father's arguments about cutting holes in walls, and together they began a new project. With scraps of half-inch plywood left over from the remodeling of the garage, they constructed a three-foot-square cube in the corner of the garage, and cut a door hole to join it to the run outside, making a bed for Max, out of the weather. Natalie contributed two old blankets for bedding, and a table mat to be nailed over the door to keep out the rain. Max nosed through, turned twice in the bedding, stirred it with his feet, and settled in appreciatively. But when David went into the house for dinner, Max clamored to go, too, and David brought him.

As each day passed with no unpleasantness between parents and dog, David relaxed another degree. Max paid little attention to Nathan or Natalie, attaching himself only to David whenever the boy was at home, and seeming to spend the rest of his time watching for David through the wire of his run.

When school began the next day, David set his alarm an hour earlier and used the time to take Max for a long jog-run out to the edge of town and back, then to clean the dog's run and fill his food and water dishes, and explain about the demands of school.

When David got home at four that afternoon, he went immediately to Max's run. The dog was lying at the far end of the run, his head turned away from David.

"Max? Are you okay?" David rushed to kneel beside the dog, thinking he was sick. Max rose and stretched and yawned, and accepted David's touch coolly.

"I had to go to school. Is that it? Are you pouting because I left you alone all day?" David was flattered, charmed. Max warmed up to him in a few minutes, and they went for their evening run. The next day Max repeated his snubbing act, but on the third day he seemed to accept the new routine. He greeted David with happy leaps against the run gate, and gamboled beside him for the first two blocks of their afternoon run.

On Friday evening David's best friend Todd called to see if David would like to go roller skating at the rink with him and his two older sisters who liked to go to the rink on Friday nights in the hope of meeting boys. The price they paid was to take Todd with them. Their parents held the belief that girls couldn't get into trouble so long as their younger brothers were with them, so Todd and David had been spending many of their Friday nights coasting around the varnished floors of Roller Town, playing chaperone with gleeful vengeance and secretly eyeing the younger girls as they rumbled past.

But tonight David passed on the invitation. Max was lying across his foot again, and David thought about all of the hours this week when Max had had to wait for him while he was in school. It didn't seem fair to leave Max again.

Natalie was at home for once, working on a macrame plant hanger she was trying to finish before her sister's birthday, and watching television while she worked. David hung up the phone and twisted back into his corner of the sofa.

"Didn't you want to go skating?" Natalie said, having heard David's end of the conversation.

"Nah, not really."

She looked up from her twists of white cord and raised her eyebrows at him. "You feeling okay?"

"Sure." David shrugged. "I just didn't feel like going skating."

"Umm." Natalie looked from him to the dog lying across his foot, but she said no more on the subject.

"Hey, Mom, look," David said a few minutes later. A commercial showed a young man and woman racing along a beach with a Doberman leaping beside them. The dog wore a bandanna knotted around his neck like a cowboy's scarf, and he was leaping into the air, catching a Frisbee.

"I wonder if Max could do that. Where'd my Frisbee go, do you remember?"

51

"Try those shelves in the pool room," Natalie muttered, her teeth full of macrame cord.

"Come on, Maxie, let's see how smart you are."

David and the dog pounded down the basement stairs. He found the red plastic disk and bounded back upstairs where there was more room.

"Here, Max, catch it." He spun the Frisbee in a slow easy arc, and the dog leaped after it.

"Be careful of the lamps," Natalie warned, but she watched with interest as Max made one catch after another. Sometimes he missed, but after half a dozen tries the dog began to make more intelligent approaches, snatching at the spinning disc from the side as it sailed past his head.

"He really is smart, Mom," David insisted.

"I never said he wasn't smart. I just don't trust him."

"Oh, you will after a while," David said confidently. It was going to be all right. He was beginning to be almost positive Max was going to be all right. David sank back onto the sofa and wrapped his arm around Max's neck while Max rested his chin on David's knee. The dog's eyes closed slowly, lulled by the rhythm of David's stroking palm.

He'd be dead by now if it wasn't for me, David thought. *I gave him his life. I'm giving him his happiness, taking care of him and playing with him, taking him for runs. I'm the most important person in the world to him.*

A slow smile spread across his face. For the first time in years his thoughts touched on Corky without pain. Okay, a failure there, but he was making up for it now. One dog dead because of David, but another one alive. It felt good. *Oh,* it felt good.

52

The next morning David rushed through his Saturday chores, cleaning his room and changing the sheets on his bed and mowing the lawn, which only took half an hour because the grass hadn't really begun to grow yet so the densely shaded parts of the lawn could be skipped. Then for the first time, he turned Max loose in the back yard.

He held his breath and called the dog frequently, but Max was perfect. He trotted the circumference of the back yard and sniffed everything and lifted his leg to mark his territory, but whenever David called, Max came directly to him, with no sign of the cringing he had done with Sally.

David got the Frisbee from the house and sailed it through the air. Max tore after it, leaping, snatching, usually catching and returning it to David when he did. It occurred to David that this was perfect, according to Sally's rules. It was great exercise for the dog, less work and time for David than running was, and it was relaxing and fun, without the pressures of formal training. An ideal way to deprogram Max, to relax him and make him forget his attack training. "I hope," David said aloud.

The next day, eager to have other people see and admire his beautiful dog, David packed sandwiches and the Frisbee in his backpack book bag, snapped on Max's leash, and biked out the highway to Sally's house. There was no one home. Dog shows, probably, David thought, disappointed. Back to town they pedaled, but not home. It was a perfect spring Sunday, and he had a wonderful dog, and he wanted to be out with people, showing off.

They went to the small neighborhood park where

they had picnicked the week before, and David sat on a rustic bench to eat his lunch. Then he took Max to the far end of the park, away from the busy playground area to a place of grass and clumps of trees and underbrush. A wooded ravine cut across this corner of the park. Beyond it was civilization and sidewalks, but the ravine gave a sense of wild country.

David unsnapped Max's leash and lay down his backpack, taking out the Frisbee and showing it to Max.

"Here we go, Maxie. Catch it."

It was a high, clean, beautiful spin, and Max had to leap to catch it, just like the dog in last night's commercial. David laughed aloud at the pleasure of the moment. He threw again, even higher and farther this time.

The Frisbee sailed in among the trees of the ravine. Max plunged after it. David waited, trusting Max. A minute passed.

"He must be having a hard time finding . . ."

David thought he heard a faint high yelp. Uneasiness stirred in his stomach. He started across the grass toward the ravine. Max was there, plunging down the opposite slope toward David, bringing him the red Frisbee . . . no. No!

Not a Frisbee. Oh, God. Max's eyes glittered as he placed his gift at David's feet. It was a small dog, mophaired and cat-sized, and dead. Blood dripped from its mouth; its eyes were already drying horribly.

"Oh, Max," David keened. "Why did you?"

The dog lowered his head, puzzled by David's tone.

"Snookie, come Snookie." From the far side of the ravine a woman's voice called.

"Oh, God." David's thoughts careened in his head. If

Max were caught with this, it would be the end of him. David couldn't face it. Without thinking he swooped and picked up the little dog and plunged up the wooded bank. "Come on, Max. We've got to get out of here."

Out in the sunlight again they ran to David's backpack and he stuffed the little corpse inside. Then, his hands shaking, he snapped on Max's leash and headed back toward the playground and his bike. He thought he might be sick, but it didn't quite happen. The backpack made a horrible bulge against his back as David mounted his bike and began pedaling toward home.

Get rid of it. Get rid of it. How? Where? Go back and leave it in the ravine. The owner will find it and know not to keep looking. She probably loved her little dog just like I love Max.

David's eyes filled with tears. He knew this to be the worst moment in his life. He knew the right thing to do: go back and find the woman who was calling her dog, tell her what happened, apologize, offer to pay for the little dog.

But he couldn't. He simply couldn't face doing that, couldn't face the woman with such terrible news, couldn't face the rage she would feel against Max, couldn't face the inevitable death sentence this would mean for Max.

At the next corner there was a city trash container. David paused beside it, pretending to fiddle with his bike chain, until he was sure no cars were coming, no faces watching from nearby windows. Then, trembling and sick at what he was doing, he emptied the backpack into the trash barrel. There was a forlorn thump inside as the little dog's body landed among the candy

55

wrappers and cigarette packs and hardened wads of gum.

A few days later when Natalie asked David where the Frisbee had gone, he muttered that he'd lost it in the park. In those days David often took Max's head between his hands and stared into the dog's eyes, and tested whether he could still love a dog who had done such a terrible thing.

He found he could, and did. It would have been easier if he hadn't.

7

It was a muggy morning in July. David woke late and stretched his legs to find Max, a heavy, warm weight across the foot of the bed. The dog stirred and lifted his head and turned his golden eyes on David, then crawled up the boy's body to stare more closely into his face as though affirming that David was indeed awake.

"Hey, Maxie, we're a couple of lazy bums this morning, aren't we?" David wrapped his arm around the dog and pulled him into a hug, and Max settled his throat over David's, crisscrossed as puppies do for warmth and protection. David giggled and pretended to choke, and shoved Max away.

"Come on, bum." He rolled up out of bed and pulled on his denim cutoffs. "What shall we do today, go out to Sally's?"

They went through the cool lower rooms of the house and out the back door. While Max was lifting his leg on each of his marking points around the edge of the yard, David glanced at Max's run and noticed fresh claw marks in the dirt just inside the fence. The grass within the run had long since disappeared, leaving hard packed earth, and now these signs of excavation. *Uh-oh,* David thought.

He and Max went back into the house. Natalie was already gone for the day, deep in her summer school classes, but Nathan was at the refectory table at the end of the kitchen, drinking coffee, reading the morning paper, and dodging the caresses of a tendril of Swedish ivy dangling near his ear.

David poured himself a glass of milk, found a doughnut that was still edible from the bakery box on the counter, and sat down across from his father. Max settled into his spot near David's foot.

"Dad?"

"Mmm."

"Are you home this morning?"

"No, son, this is an android cleverly fashioned to resemble your father and equipped with an answering device for recorded messages. At the sound of the tone, please leave your message and I will return your call."

"Come on, Dad."

Nathan emerged from the newspaper, smiling but unshaven.

"I'm home in that I haven't left yet, but I'm not home for the day. Does that answer your question? I have to be in court at one. Why?"

"I was just noticing, it looks like Max has been digging in his run, like he was trying to dig out."

"Uh-oh," Nathan said.

"That's what I said. Can we do something about it?"

Nathan frowned. "I expect we'd better. Leash laws aside, I still don't trust Max. I know he's your dog and you love him, and so far he's been okay . . ."

David's thoughts flashed to the little dead dog in Max's jaws.

". . . but I still don't trust him, and I sure don't want

the responsibility of his getting loose. Let's see. I'd have time to run you over to the lumberyard and pick up a roll of chicken wire or something like that. You'll have to dig a trench all around the run and bury it. I won't have time to help with that."

David nodded. He swallowed the last of his doughnut past a thickening in his throat and said, "Dad, you defend the underdogs a lot, in court, don't you?"

Nathan laughed. "Max was the first one I ever defended that had four legs and a tail, though."

"Seriously, Dad."

"Seriously. Yes. I do. That's why I chose to become a public defender instead of a rich lawyer with carpet on his office floor."

"Why did you?"

Nathan stared down into his coffee cup and shrugged. "It seemed like a good idea at the time. No, that's a straight question and I'll give it a straight answer. Yes, I guess the underdog has always appealed to me. I probably have a savior complex or something. I like the idea of saving people for whom I'm their only hope. The rich clients can get anyone. They don't need me as much as the poor guy who is definitely going to get the short end of the judicial system unless I'm good at my job. Does that make any sense to you? Were you thinking about going that direction with your career?"

David hunched his shoulders around his ears. "No, that wasn't what I was thinking about right now. I was thinking about Max."

Nathan sat quietly, waiting, but David couldn't think how to frame his thoughts into words that anyone would understand.

"Dad, what happens when you defend somebody like

that and get them off, and then it turns out they really were guilty?"

"That happens sometimes. All I can do is give my client the best legal advice and defense I can. The rest is out of my hands."

"I know that, but what if you get some murderer off, say for instance, and then he goes out and kills somebody else? Don't you feel responsible for that?"

Nathan looked more closely at his son. "What are we talking about here, Dave?"

David shrugged deeply and looked down.

Nathan pressed, "Are you worried about Max? Is that what we're talking about?"

"No. I was just asking. Yeah, you were right, I was thinking about my career. That's all."

They dropped the subject, but rode more quietly than usual to the lumberyard, Max sitting upright as a sentry in the back seat. They bought a fifty-foot roll of eighteen-inch-wide chicken mesh and hog rings to fasten the wire to the chain link, and added eighteen dollars to the slowly diminishing amount David still owed for the building of the run.

When they got home David let Max out of the car, then took one end of the fencing roll and began walking backward, helping Nathan carry it.

"Watch your—"

David tripped, stumbled, fell backward with a laughing whoop, and Nathan stumbled on his foot, lost his balance, and fell across David and the fence roll.

Before they could catch their breaths and sort out enough legs to stand on, Max was upon them, snarling, diving for Nathan's throat.

"No," David screamed. "Down, Max. No!"

"Christ," Nathan breathed. He lay sprawled on his back, half over the mashed roll of wire, his face white with fear. Max stood astride him, forefeet on Nathan's shoulders, bared teeth inches away from Nathan's face.

David scrambled toward them and grabbed Max's chain collar. "*No*, Max. Get off. Get back."

The rumbling in the dog's throat gradually died, but David could feel it vibrating still, through the collar. The glitter of madness began to fade from the dog's eyes, and the black lips gradually eased forward to cover his fangs.

"Get back, damn you," David yelled, jerking the dog off of his father and fighting tears and trembling. In that instant he hated Max with all his heart.

Slowly, carefully, Nathan climbed to his feet.

"Are you okay, Dad?" David could barely get the words out, so shaken was his voice.

"Yeah. I guess. Put him in his pen." Abruptly Nathan turned and walked toward the house. David ran to lock up Max, then to catch up with his father.

"I'm sorry, Dad. He didn't mean it. He must have thought you were attacking me, when you fell on me like that and we both yelled. He just made a mistake, Dad."

At the back door, Nathan turned and looked at David. "Yes. A mistake. Very nearly a fatal one, Davie. That can't happen again. I'm afraid of that dog, and you would be too if you weren't so crazy about him."

David stood very still. "He would never hurt me. Max wouldn't. He loves me."

"He just now made a mistake," Nathan said in a heavy, level tone. "He could make another one. I think

61

you need to give some serious thought to your responsibilities here, son."

"Max is my responsibility."

Nathan just looked at him, then turned and went into the house.

David worked until early afternoon, digging a foot-deep trench around the base of the run, then burying a strip of the chicken wire fencing in the trench and stapling the top of the wire to the chain link with the hog rings. Then, since there was half the roll left, he fastened the rest of the wire around the top of the run, bracing it at the corners with scraps of wood, to discourage any ideas Max might get about climbing over when he couldn't dig out under.

He went into the house, leaving Max to test the new security of the run while he washed and warmed up a dish of leftover casserole for his lunch. It was only a little after two. He decided to ride out to Sally's house. He'd become a regular visitor there, drawn by the woman's warmth and straightforwardness.

The day was growing cloudy and close, the damp air blowing against David's skin but not cooling him. He found Sally in the training ring behind the barn-kennel.

She raised her hand in greeting, but went on working the dog at her side, polishing his about-turns so that the dog whipped about in a smart U-turn that would lose no scoring points in competition. David sat in the grass, enjoying his momentary freedom from the tension of Max.

After a while Sally came out of the ring and dropped beside him. The dog she'd been working came to David, grinning and wagging and eager for a hug.

"Who's this?" David said, studying the dog's face. He

was still confused about the identity of some of the Goldens, so many of them looked alike. This one looked very much like a younger version of Bear.

"This is Mister T. I just got him back a couple of days ago. Whew, this is no weather to be training dogs. You could drink this air. Storm coming, or I'm a monkey's aunt."

"Got him back? From where?"

"Oh"—Sally wiped the sweat from her face with her shirttail and fanned herself with the dog's lead—"I sold him as a puppy to some people down by Burlington, because I thought he was going to be too small to do any good in the show ring. Well, they called and wanted me to take him back. They're getting a divorce and both of them are moving to apartments, so I said what the hell. I'm glad I did, too. He turned into one hell of a dog. Look at the head on him, Dave. And look at that front, those legs as straight and true as railroad tracks. I don't believe old Bear has ever produced a better son."

"Are you going to keep him then?"

She sniffed and rubbed her nose with the lead. "I'd sure love to. It's time to retire the Bear, and this old puppy would make an ideal replacement for his daddy, wouldn't you, you worthless cur?" She shoved the dog, rolled him over on the ground, and rubbed his belly with her knuckles.

"Trouble is, I don't have kennel space for two studs. So, I don't know. You need a belly rub, you worthless mutt? You like that?"

"How come dogs are always doing that?" David asked.

"What, rolling over and asking for a rub like this?

63

Actually, that's not what they're doing at all. That's the dog's signal that means they give you domination over them. Like yelling 'Uncle' in a fight."

"No kidding?"

"I never kid a kid. All the things dogs do, like that, have meaning for them. It's their language. We just don't always make the effort to learn it. Sure, when two dogs fight, they don't fight to kill each other, they fight symbolically. They raise their hackles to make themselves look bigger to the enemy. They go through the motions of fighting, but only until one or the other goes over on his back in this submissive position, then the other one lets him up and the fight's over. That doesn't go for the dogs they use in those horrible illegal dog fights, of course, those pit bulls, but they aren't normal sane dogs."

David's stomach churned. In the silence he worked his way toward telling Sally about what Max had done, but before he could get there, she lurched to her feet.

"You've never seen the old man work, have you, Dave? Want to? You wait here, I'll go get him."

She left and came back a few minutes later carrying a miniature suitcase and a bundle of white work gloves. The old dog, Bear, bounced in circles around her.

She laid the things down and went to work assembling the jumps that usually stood alongside the training ring. There was a high jump, like a segment of board fence, three feet high, in the center of the ring, and a row of low boards just inches off the ground and covering a span of six feet along the other side.

"You've already seen enough Novice-level work," Sally called. "We'll just demonstrate his Open- and

Utility-level stuff. He loves this. He loves to work, don't you, you old fool?"

Bear was circling madly around Sally's legs. "Heel," she commanded, and he settled in a perfect square sit at her left side. Then, with no further word, she motioned him forward with a scoop of her palm and they went through a heeling pattern, the dog staying perfectly aligned with Sally's left knee, through slows and fasts and quick about-turns and swift figure eights.

Then, standing in one corner of the ring, she gave him a silent stay signal and left him to cross to the opposite end. A swoop of her arm brought the dog tearing toward her; a quickly raised arm stopped him in his tracks and dropped him in a deep crouch. Another arm swoop and he completed the recall and returned to her side by leaping into the air, turning in midair, and landing sitting, in heel position. David applauded.

"Don't applaud, throw coins," Sally said, then went back to concentrating on the dog. She pulled a small wooden dumbbell from her pocket and threw it. Bear trembled with passion, but waited until she signaled before he leaped forward, pounced on the dumbbell, and raced back with it.

They moved sideways to the high jump, where Sally threw the dumbbell over the barrier and sent Bear flying over it in a perfect retrieve. Then to the broad jump, the low planks along the far side of the ring. Sally placed Bear at one end of the jump, then took her place beside the planks. With a quick "Bear, over," she released him into a beautiful extended leap that just cleared the six-foot span. The dog landed already turning, and finished in front of Sally.

"Now the fun stuff," she said as she began rearranging the jumps. She replaced the broad jump with a high pole jump and moved the other high jump to the edge of the ring. Then she picked up the miniature suitcase and walked to the center of the ring where she dumped its contents: ten small dumbbells, some of leather, some of aluminum. She picked up one of each and returned to the edge of the ring, facing David.

"He loves to do his scent articles," she said. She slipped the leather dumbbell down her shirt front and rubbed the metal one in her hands; then, giving Bear a stay command, she turned and laid the dumbbell she'd been rubbing near the untouched ones in the center of the ring.

Standing again beside Bear she said, "Bear, take *mine*," and whirled to face the dumbbells. Bear whirled with her and leaped to the nine dumbbells in the grass. Tail lashing, he examined each of the nine with his nose until he found the one with Sally's skin scent on it. This one he picked up carefully in his teeth, hating the metal taste, and brought it back to Sally.

"Good show, now the other one." They repeated the exercise with the leather dumbbell. "Go to the head of the class."

"I won't show you the signal exercises, he already did most of that before. We'll just do directed retrieving and jumping and call it a day."

Sally lay three white work gloves in a line across the far end of the ring, then pointed to the one on the right. Bear raced to retrieve it, but detoured to pick up the other two before he came back, cramming all three gloves into his jaws and looking saucy. Through David's mind again flashed the picture of Max bearing his broken victim through the ravine.

"Wrong, you rotten dog," Sally called. "He was only supposed to retrieve the one I indicated. He used to pull that all the time in the show ring. Just being cute. He knew better."

They came out of the ring and sat beside David, Bear carrying one of the gloves as his treat. "Doesn't work like an eight-year-old dog, does he? No hip dysplasia in my bloodline, boy."

"Do you think I could train Max to do stuff like that?" David asked.

Sally shrugged. "Probably, if you stayed with it long enough. He's got his basic novice work under his belt already. It would just be a matter of getting him started with jumping and retrieving. Takes a lot of work, though. Over a year for Bear, and he's a super learner, I'm an experienced trainer, and I had him in classes the whole time, through the obedience club. That helps."

"Could I get Max into a class, do you think?" The idea was growing in David's mind. The picture of Max retrieving gloves and dumbbells hurt so much less than the other picture.

"Sure, if you want. The club just started a Novice A class a couple of weeks ago. You could still get into that one, since Max is started already. You can ride with me if you want. I'm teaching the Puppy Kindergarten class."

David was quiet for a few minutes. "Sally? Would that kind of training help or hurt, do you think, with his, you know . . ."

"Deprograming the attack training?"

"Yeah."

She shrugged again. "Probably wouldn't hurt him, at this stage. He's relaxed quite a bit from what he was when you got him, hasn't he? A little structured discipline might be a good idea at this point."

David said nothing.

She nudged him with her elbow. "You're kind of quiet today, Dave. Having problems?"

"Oh, yeah, kind of. In a way. Not problems exactly . . ."

"Max?"

David nodded. "He went for my dad this morning. Dad and I were carrying a roll of fence wire and I tripped and fell, and my dad fell over me, and I guess Max thought he was attacking me or something. I didn't have any trouble pulling him off. He didn't bite or anything, but . . ."

Sally blew through her lips and gave David a long, compassionate look. "I really think you've got a tiger by the tail with that dog, if you want my honest opinion. I know that's not what you want to hear, but . . ." She shook her head.

They were quiet again for a long time, then David said in a low voice. "I'd like to try the obedience classes."

"Sure, Tuesday evenings in Elmwood Park. I'll pick you up about six-thirty. And David, if I were you I wouldn't mention the fact that Max is attack trained around that class. I don't think he'd be welcomed with very open arms."

David pedaled home, feeling rotten.

8

The house was empty when David got home. He got a can of Coke from the refrigerator and went out to Max's run, where the dog was waiting, pacing and leaping against the wire. When David opened the run gate, Max bounded out and flung himself against David's chest, his eyes alight with the joy of the reunion.

"I've only been gone a couple of hours," David said, setting down his Coke can and rolling on the ground with Max. The dog leaped up, tore in circles around the yard, and finally came back to press his body against David's, panting.

As David stroked the hard black coat, the bony head, he saw again his father lying on the ground with Max at his throat. This dog, whose eyes shone with love for David, had threatened to kill David's father. The thought sickened David, and his mind veered away from it.

He thought about Bear flying over his jumps, retrieving his dumbbells and delivering them with gay devotion into Sally's hand. If only Max . . .

If only Max was like Bear. Pure pleasure without the fear. The thought made David feel disloyal, and he pressed Max's head closer to his chest, stroked it

69

harder. Max was his dog, and whatever had been done to Max by whoever trained him to attack human beings, whatever damage had been done to this beautiful creature's mind, it was David Purdy's job to undo. If love was enough, love and patience and obedience lessons, then Max would come out of it. Someday, someday Max would be like Bear.

A small flicker of knowledge at the back of his mind warned him that he was fooling himself. He shut it out and concentrated on the obedience lessons. They would do the trick. They had to. An obedience-trained dog, maybe even a winner of an obedience trial, nobody would be afraid of a dog like that, would they? Parents wouldn't be afraid.

David refused to acknowledge that some of the fear he feared was his own.

He stayed in the back yard until both of his parents were home. Their voices floated out to him through the kitchen window but he stayed away from them, stayed with Max. He commanded Max to heel, and they walked and ran around the yard, turning and stopping together.

At first Max ranged several feet away from David's side, but gradually he got better at it; he seemed to remember old lessons.

Nathan called, "David, supper."

Throughout the meal there were silences among the three, stiff silences that made David sense trouble. Natalie's eyes kept darting downward toward Max, who lay in his usual place under the table, chin on David's foot.

Finally the eating slowed to a stop and Natalie said, "We've got to have a little family conference here."

David felt heavy with dread.

Nathan said, "Son, I told your mom what happened this morning, with Max, and we both feel that we've let this situation go on long enough. Too long, probably."

"But he didn't bite you. He didn't actually bite you. He thought he was protecting me, Dad. Just for that flash there, he thought you were hurting me, and he was trying to protect me."

"The point is," Natalie said, "Max is dangerous. He is a risk waiting to explode, and we just don't feel we can go on keeping him."

"But I love him." David fought tears.

Nathan said, "We know you do, Davie, and we feel terrible about this. It's my fault for letting you have him in the first place. I wish . . ."

"But you did. You said I could have him, and he's my dog and I love him, and now you want to make me kill him like you did Corky." David's voice was high and shrill. It echoed in the sudden stillness of the kitchen.

In his own rage David couldn't see the pain in his mother's face. He shouted, "Why do you keep giving me dogs and then making me kill them?"

Nathan said, "Now settle down, son. Nobody said anything about killing Max."

"No, but what else . . ." David stopped, not wanting to say, "What else could be done with a vicious dog?"

Instead he said, "I went out to Sally's this afternoon, and I was telling her about what happened, and she said I should take Max to obedience classes. That would probably settle him down just fine, you know, give him something to do with his energy, something for him to think about. They've got classes that just started, on

71

Tuesday nights, and she said I could take Max. And I want to. Really badly."

Nathan looked sternly into David's eyes. "Sally actually said that obedience lessons would make Max a safe animal to have around?"

David faltered, dropped his gaze. "Well, she didn't exactly say that, in so many words, but she thought it would help a lot. And she thought he'd be good at it. He's so smart."

Nathan opened his mouth to argue, but Natalie interrupted. "Hon, let's think about this a minute. Maybe we could hold off a little bit. David's right; as Max is now we'd have a problem getting rid of him. We couldn't honestly sell or even give away a dog we knew to be dangerous. It wouldn't be ethical. The only alternative we'd have would be to have Max put down, and none of us wants to go through another experience like Corky."

David looked at his mother, startled by the idea that Corky's death might have been an ordeal for anyone but himself. Especially for his mother, whom he had always cast as the iron-hearted executioner.

Quickly he said, "How about if we did this? How about if I take him to the obedience classes, and we'll just see if it makes any difference in his temperament. It'll be eight weeks till the classes are over, and if he still seems like he might be dangerous after that, then we'll—"

Nathan said firmly, "Then we'll have him put down, humanely of course, but we will have him put down."

David rushed on. "Yes, but if he does really well in the classes and doesn't cause any more trouble, then I can keep him?"

His father and mother exchanged a long look, in which they read the subtle facial language of a closely bonded couple. It was Natalie who spoke. "It's a deal. But David, one thing that's important here. Listen now. If it ends up that Max does have to be put down, I don't want any one of us to blame any other one of us, even in our hearts. I don't want you blaming me or your father for the death penalty, and certainly no one should blame you for failing Max in any way. Do you think you can be mature enough to go into it with that attitude?"

Solemn-faced but with spirit lifting, David nodded.

9

On Tuesday night David and Max were in the front yard, waiting, well before six-thirty. David wore his best knit polo shirt, and his hair was neatly combed; Max had been brushed to a high gloss. David was eager for the training class, for his introduction into Iowa City's dog show crowd. And he was nervous about Max, about his ability to control the dog around that many strange people and dogs.

As they stood near the curb watching for Sally's car, a girl on a bike coasted down a driveway across the street and rolled to a stop beside David. It was Joyce Bates, whom David was beginning to dislike actively.

She stopped her bike and sat with legs outstretched, bracing herself and rocking the bike from side to side as she stared down at Max. She was a thin-lipped, mousy-haired child with skinny, scabby brown legs and a rim of dirt near her mouth, an aged milk mustache.

"I don't like that dog," she announced flatly.

David tightened his grip on Max's leather lead. "Tough toenails. He doesn't like you either."

Joyce made a face at Max.

She glanced at David, taunting, then whooshed her arms toward Max as though to snatch at him. The dog rumbled low in his throat; David felt it vibrating up the lead.

"Joyce, knock it off. You tease this dog and you're going to wish you hadn't. I'm not kidding now."

"He's ugly."

"So are you," David retorted.

"So are you, fatty."

Sally's station wagon coasted to a stop behind Joyce's bike, and David turned toward it with relief. Sally got out and swung the tailgate open. In the back of the car were two wire-mesh dog crates, an empty one and one holding a reclining Golden.

"Is that Mister T?" David asked as Sally opened the door to the empty crate and David boosted Max into it.

"Yep. I've got him entered in some August and September shows, in Conformation. Thought I'd enter him in Novice Obedience, too, as long as I was hauling him. A few practice sessions at these Tuesday night classes and he should be ready. His other owners trained him."

They got into the car and drove away. Sally said, "You'll have to work Mister T for me if I'm tied up with my PK class, okay?"

"Sure." David grinned.

He stopped grinning when they pulled into the park. It was the same park where Max had killed the little dog. The name of the park hadn't registered when Sally mentioned it earlier. David's stomach soured as he released Max from the crate and followed Sally across the grass to a flat, open area where several people and dogs were gathered.

"Ozzie," Sally called, "I got a new student for your Novice A class. This is David Purdy, he's a friend of mine. His Dobe has already had some training. I think he'll be able to keep up with the rest of the class."

Ozzie was a small man, bald and gray-bearded, with wire-rim glasses riding low on his nose and an elfin expression. He smiled at David, let the smile drop to include Max, and rubbed his hand quickly over Max's skull. The dog leaned against David's leg but made no protest.

"Glad to have you, David. Hi there, Max. Okay, you've got the right kind of collar and lead, and your collar's on right-side up. So far you're ahead of the game. We're about ready to start."

Ozzie wandered off, consulting a list on the clipboard on his arm. Sally had already gone a short distance away and begun gathering her PK class around her. David watched as she rounded up the dozen puppy owners and sat them in a circle on the ground, with their puppies in the center of the circle, playing and sniffing and rolling one another over.

"Novice A class, over here," Ozzie yelled. "Let's see, we've got Ace and Toby and Peanut and Schatzie and Starsky, where's . . . oh, there he is, Ralph the Poodle, and Max. Okay, form a circle and we'll start off with a little heeling practice."

David fell in with the others, staying as far away from the other dogs as he could. For several minutes he circled with the others, keeping Max even with his left leg and following Ozzie's shouted commands to forward, halt, fast, slow, about-turn. Max concentrated on the work at hand and paid little attention to the other dogs. Gradually David began to relax and enjoy himself.

They practiced sit-stays, with the handlers standing at the far end of their leashes, facing their sitting dogs.

76

Max was better at it than most of the others. While the dogs were sitting, David glanced at the other dogs in the class: one other Doberman, a miniature wirehaired dachshund, three shelties, a huge black standard poodle, and a Golden who was not nearly as beautiful as Sally's dogs, in David's opinion.

Next they practiced the down-stay. Again, Max was obedient though reluctant, fighting the idea of lying down completely. Ralph the Poodle had to be thrown down and lain across by his puffing handler, and the miniature dachshund snapped at its owner's hands as the woman tried to maneuver him down into the grass. David felt better and better about Max.

After another several minutes of heeling practice, the class was dismissed so that the handlers who had more than one dog could work their second dogs. Glancing at Sally, David saw that she was still busy with her puppy class, so he put Max back into his crate in the open-doored wagon, and took out Mister T.

There were only four of them now, the young woman who had had the other Doberman in Max's class and who now was working with a different Dobe, a brown and red one, one of the sheltie handlers with a different dog, and Ralph the Poodle, back for another session since his high spirits were only beginning to be subdued after the first half-hour class.

Heeling with Mister T, David was amazed at the difference between this dog and Max. Although they were similar in height and the Golden was considerably broader, Mister T was much lighter on the lead than Max had been. He seemed to float along beside David with none of the muscular tension that Max radiated. David enjoyed himself absolutely.

77

It was becoming too dark to see clearly, and the mosquitoes were plaguing by the time Sally dismissed her puppy class and Ozzie called, "That's enough, see you next week." Glancing across the park toward the wooded ravine, David realized he'd gotten through the entire training session without serious worries about controlling Max. He felt great.

As the group started toward their respective wagons and vans, Ozzie said to Sally, "Burger Chef?"

"You bet."

They drove out of the residential area onto Highway 218 and into the parking lot of the Burger Chef. "This is your reward for training my dog tonight," Sally said.

"Yay." David scratched the mosquito bites on his arm.

Inside, the restaurant was almost empty except for the large circular booth in the corner, already almost filled with people from the training class. They shifted into a more tightly packed mass to make room for David and Sally. People smiled at David and went on with their conversations. David ordered a chocolate malt, Sally a cheeseburger and Coke.

Tired, pleased with himself and with Max, and deeply happy to be included in this good-natured group of dog people, David sat back and inhaled his malt and listened to the voices around him.

"So I said look, lady, if you want a seventy-five dollar dog you go someplace else because you're not going to get one here. My God, Purina Hi Pro is up to almost twenty dollars a bag, show entries fifteen bucks, cost you a good two, three thousand to finish a champion anymore, and people expect to buy champion-sired puppies for seventy-five . . ."

". . . entered him in the American Bred class. I told him you don't ever enter a dog in American Bred, you're just telling the judge you don't think he's good enough for Open, but does he ever listen to me? Hell no . . ."

". . . reading an article on swimmer puppies. Mary Jo, didn't you have a swimmer in that litter you had last summer? Anyhow, this article said it's not a calcium deficiency at all, it's that the pups are on newspapers, where they can't get a grip. Said, put your litter on blankets or something like that, and the swimmer's chest will fill right out. Try it next time."

David whispered to Sally, "What's a swimmer?"

"Newborn pup that's flattened out like a turtle."

His eyes widened.

Ozzie said, "Anybody here get a call from some guy out by Mt. Vernon with a Rottweiler he wants to attack train?"

The booth fell silent. David shrank.

Ozzie went on. "Some guy called me the other night, said he wanted to get his dog into the club's training classes, then asked if we did attack training. Honestly," he snorted.

The young woman with the Dobermans said, "What'd you tell him?"

"I says we don't touch any kind of attack or guard training. I says this is an obedience club and we wouldn't go near that stuff."

Snorts around the table. David concentrated on the malt in his glass.

Ozzie went on. "I asked the guy what he wanted an attack-trained Rott for, and he said to protect his kids."

Cynical laughter rippled around the table.

"So who's going to protect the kids from the attack dog?"

"Send the fox to guard the henhouse."

"Some of those attack-dog trainers get two, three thousand dollars for their dogs. What a rip-off."

"Wish I could get that for my good show puppies. I'm lucky to get three hundred."

The talk became general again, and David relaxed a fraction. Sally patted his knee, and he knew she'd been feeling his pain, and sympathizing.

10

For the next few weeks David's days centered on the training sessions. Before breakfast, while the morning air was cool and damp with absorbed dew, he and Max worked together in the back yard, first playing chasing games with tossed sticks to wear the edge off Max's exuberance, then getting down to serious business.

Around and across the yard they heeled, halted, about-turned, sped up, slowed down, always working toward precision closeness. They practiced sit-stay and down-stay for longer and longer periods of time until Max became dependable for several minutes in a row.

In the evenings when Nathan and Natalie were available to help, they worked again, this time heeling in tight figure-eights around the patiently standing parents. Max was inclined to sniff at Nathan's knees as he circled past him, and to shrink away from close contact with Natalie.

There were no more incidents of threat from the dog. He seemed to enjoy the training sessions, and by the third week he had begun to know that Tuesday night was class night and to respond to that knowledge. As six-thirty approached on that third Tuesday, Max grew agitated, pacing through the house on staccato toenails and peering out the front window, whining, while David was changing clothes.

When Sally's car pulled to a stop in front of the house that night, it was Bear rather than Mister T in the crate. "Mister T's got a huge hot spot on his side," she explained. "That's an eczema, you know, big patch of raw skin. They get it a lot, this time of year. He looked so awful I didn't want to bring him. And Ozzie was wanting me to bring Bear and do a Utility demonstration, so I thought this would be a good night to do that."

David's class was already working when they pulled into the park. He snapped Max's leash on as the dog jumped down from the crate, and together they ran to make a place for themselves in the circle of heeling dogs. When everyone had practiced heeling and the come-on-recall exercise they had begun learning the previous week, Ozzie motioned them to a halt.

"This week we'll start on the stand for examination exercise," he said, and demonstrated the correct way to stand the dog. "Now you all try it."

Concentrating on Ozzie's instructions, David walked Max up out of sitting position, said, "Max, stand," and bent to place his hand against the dog's flank.

Max lowered his head and growled. Startled, David pulled back and Max sat down.

"Make him stand," Ozzie called. "Remember who's boss."

Again David walked Max a step forward, commanded him to stand, and braced him under the flank. Again Max lowered his head, glared at David, and rumbled a warning. This time he didn't sit, but stood in a humped position, his eyes glittering at David from his low-held head.

From the center of the ring Ozzie said, "Okay now, you've all got your dogs in standing position, give them the stay command, and I'll come around and touch them, see how many of them will hold still for that."

Please, please, David begged Max with his eyes. Ozzie approached and reached to touch the dog's humped back. Max snarled and made a lightning snap at Ozzie's wrist. The man jerked back, startled.

"Correct him when he does that," Ozzie said. "Don't ever let him get away with growling or snapping at anyone, or you're going to have a problem on your hands." Ozzie moved on to the next dog.

David shrank into himself and went woodenly through the motions of finishing the class, then put Max back into the car crate and slammed the door. He didn't want to watch the second session of his class working, and he especially did not want to watch Bear going through his Utility routine for Sally, leaping and retrieving, tossing his glove in the air and thrashing his plumed tail in delight at Sally's praise. At that moment David could bear neither his own dog nor the one who was what he so passionately wanted his own dog to be like.

During the next two weeks David was careful never to practice the stand for examination exercise when either of his parents might be watching. But practice it he did, with grim determination, and gradually Max began to relax. By the end of the second week Max was standing readily on command, although he still bared his teeth when Ozzie attempted to touch him. The instructor could pet Max at any other time, before or after class, but for reasons that only Max knew, the dog grew tense on the stand-stay command and refused to allow any hands but David's to approach him.

"It must have been something that happened to him when he was first trained," David said, "before I got him."

Ozzie scratched his cheek and said, "Could have been, you never know. Some dogs just feel insecure in stand-stay position, like some of them feel insecure in down position. All I can say is, practice with as many different people as you can when you work him at home. He's going to be the best-scoring dog in this class by graduation night, if you can just get him past this one hang-up."

"Would he be good enough to show in regular obedience trials, and get his CD degree, do you think?"

"Oh yeah, sure. Easily. If you can get him steady on the stand. Preferably without drawing blood." Ozzie grinned and moved away.

The next evening, knowing he could put it off no longer, David put Max on stand-stay after Nathan and Natalie had done their usual stint as figure-eight posts.

"Okay now," he said to his father, "you play like you're the judge, just walk up to him and run your hand down him, from his head to his rump, and then just back away. Okay now, Max, you *stand*. You *stay*." His voice crackled under the pressure of the moment.

Nathan approached. Max's head dropped. David could feel the growl vibrating through the leash. Uneasily Nathan hesitated.

"You don't have to if you don't want to," David said in a low voice. He could see the fear in his father's face. Vividly he saw Max's teeth slashing at Ozzie's wrist, at Nathan's throat. He knew that if Nathan backed away now, Max would be the victor, and would threaten anyone else who tried to touch him on the stand-stay. He wouldn't graduate at the top of his class; he wouldn't win his CD title.

He wouldn't earn the right to stay alive.

But David understood his father's fear. He felt ripples of it, himself. It was too much to ask his father to do for him.

Natalie watched tensely from a few yards away. "Nate, watch out for him. Don't . . ."

Nathan looked directly into David's eyes. "This is important, isn't it?"

It was more statement than question. David opened his mouth to answer but couldn't.

Nathan moved closer and reached toward Max.

The dog lowered his head an inch, and deepened his growl.

"Bad dog." David jerked the leash and snarled in his most savage tone.

Max froze.

Nathan's fingers touched the black skull. They moved down the rigidly arched neck, over withers and back and croup, and safely away!

To a casual observer, the rejoicing by three people and a dog would have seemed out of all proportion to the simplicity of the achievement.

August passed on slow steamy days. David worked Max harder and harder, driven by his determination to win the high-score trophy on graduation night, the night of the last training class. The trophy itself would be nothing more than a fancy glass jar filled with homemade dog biscuits, but the achievement of winning the class had become intensely important to David. Although he knew in the logical part of his mind that Max's future didn't depend on winning the class, but on behavior that reflected the dog's safeness, David knew that winning the class would be an achievement, for himself, that nothing could ever take away.

Deep below his conscious thoughts was a belief that Max was not going to be forever, that he would lose Max. He needed something to hold on to when that time came, even something as inconsequential as having trained the best dog in a small, informal obedience class.

And so the August days were filled with Max and training sessions and dog books. Much of Sally's library had found its way into David's bedroom, and the long summer afternoons passed with David and Max stretched out against each other on David's bed, dog sleeping, boy reading.

He absorbed half a dozen books on various obedience training methods and another dozen on breeding, showing, the mechanics of canine gait, the genetics of dog breeding, even a book on kennel architecture.

In spite of the August heat and David's mounting tension, there were no more problems with Max's training. Although he lowered his head and stiffened when Nathan or others touched him on the stand-stay command, he neither growled nor bared his teeth.

It began to appear that the worst was over. When Sally gave David a sheaf of entry forms for September obedience trials, Nathan said, "Go ahead and enter him if you can pay the entry fees, and if Sally will take you."

Nathan and Natalie exchanged coded looks again, and slowly Natalie nodded her assent.

11

On graduation night David got ready early, snapped on Max's leash, and went into the front yard to wait for Sally. Natalie had just left to go to her teaching assistant's wedding shower, but promised to be at the park in time to watch David's class. Nathan was barefoot in the driveway, his pants rolled above his knees as he washed the car.

David sat on the front steps and took Max's head in his hands. "Now listen, you. You hold still and settle down. This is our big night and you'd better not blow it. We're going to get that high-score trophy, and then we're going to go to some dog shows and get you a Companion Dog title, and everybody is going to forget you ever did anything bad. You hear me?"

The dog seemed electrically wired tonight, even more keenly on edge than on other Tuesday nights. His amber eyes glittered, his heart seemed to be racing when David stroked his ribs. Tension trembled through his muscles; he was on tiptoe, straining against David, then pulling away from him.

When Nathan turned off the hose to chamois the windows, David said, "Are you coming over later to watch?"

"I plan to. I'm about done here."

Unspoken between them was the fact that there was no real reason for David to ride with Sally when his father was coming to watch the graduation night exercises. David couldn't bring himself to say anything because it was intensely important to him to be included with Sally and the others, to go to the Burger Chef after class and crowd into the corner booth with Ozzie and Mary Jo and everybody and be an adult with them for that good, warm laughing time.

He sensed that Nathan already knew this and accepted it. David felt a spreading glow of gratitude toward his father for knowing so much and saying so little.

Max lunged, pulling David up onto his feet. He barked furiously at an approaching bicycle curving up onto the lawn. It was Todd, carrying a long, flat carton, longer than the boy.

"Shut up, Max, it's only Todd, for heaven's sake. What you got there?" he called, hauling Max in and going toward the carton, which Todd laid on the grass. Todd was a tall, thin boy with a strikingly narrow face almost completely covered with freckles. His hair was dark red and kinky.

"Early birthday present," Todd said, opening the carton. "I been trying to call you. Don't you ever answer your phone?"

"I guess we didn't hear it over the hose noise. Who's it from?"

"My uncle Greg. You remember him, the one from Seattle that used to be a forest ranger? He always sends the neatest presents. Wait till you see. . . . There, isn't that a beauty?"

89

He lifted aloft a target bow, a curve of gleaming polished ash, with black leather grip and ornate sights.

"Wow."

"That's what I said. Here, give it a heft. And here's the arrows, aren't they something? See that brass tip on there? And feel the balance of it."

David lifted the arrow and balanced it on his fingers, never having felt one before. Nathan wiped his hands on his hips and came for a look, too.

"I used to do some archery in college," he said. "Let me have a look at that rascal. That's a, what, twenty pounder? Nice, nice. String it up, Todd, let's get a feel of it."

Sally's car appeared at the end of the block, and for an instant David regretted having to leave.

Todd said, "My dad's going to get me some straw bales to build a target in the backyard. Come over Saturday . . ."

David knelt and slipped Max's leash under his shoe so he could take a turn at testing the pull of the bowstring. Sally's car coasted to a stop.

At that instant Joyce Bates pedaled past, fast, on her bike. Max barked furiously and leaped to chase her.

The leash jerked free from David's foot.

"Max, no!" David commanded, starting after the dog, the arrow forgotten in his hand.

But Max was several yards ahead and flying toward the girl on the bike. He leaped and crashed mid-air with Joyce and bike.

She screamed.

The sound triggered a response in the dog that went beyond chase lust.

Horrified, David flung himself onto the tangled pile

of girl and bike and snarling dog. Blood appeared. Joyce screamed a high, thin scream that ceased abruptly.

David screamed, too, but he didn't know it. He clawed for a grip on leash, on collar. The dog was an insane beast, teeth bared horribly and flashing, slashing at the girl's face and neck.

David pulled at the dog's collar, and suddenly he fell backward to the ground, the dog now on top of him. The amber eyes were glazed with madness. Bloodied fangs filled David's vision.

Faster than thought, the hand clenching the arrow stabbed. Panic powered the fist. The factory-sharp brass tip punctured skin, bore between ribs.

The dog stiffened, went slack, fell across David's face. The world spun and faded.

David came back to the keening of a siren. Hands and arms were around him. Someone in the background was screaming, David didn't know who. The weight of the dog had been pulled away from him, but he was dizzy, unfocused.

Strangers maneuvered him onto a stretcher; a metal door slid past his eyes. Someone said, "I'm sorry, sir, there's no room back here. You and the lady will have to follow in your car."

David struggled to sit up, but weakness and hands prevented him. "Joyce?"

"She's right here with you," a man close to David's head said. "She's alive. And you're not bad hurt; I think just a little shock, mostly. You lie back now and keep that blanket over you."

"Max," David cried weakly.

"Shhh now, just lie back."

From a distance he was aware of a needle entering his arm, then he faded away again.

When he awoke he was on a narrow rolling table-bed, in a curtained area of a large, busy room. The hospital, he realized. He'd never been inside one before. A green-coated young man was bending close to his face, smoothing a bandage onto his cheek. Near his feet David could see his father in his car-washing clothes, and Sally and Todd, all staring at him with sober stiff faces.

"Joyce?" he asked.

Sally said, "She's alive. She should pull through, David. She's got some bad wounds, deep, face and throat and arms, but they've got the bleeding stopped now."

Nathan said in a shaky voice, "You saved her life, Dave."

David shook his head and met his father's eyes with his own, tear-brimmed. He looked at Sally and saw in her face the reflection of his own horror. "I didn't save her life," he whispered. "It was my fault in the first place. Everybody told me . . . Max . . ."

"You can sit up now," the doctor said. "See if you can stand."

David slid his feet toward the floor and tried to stand on them. Dizzy, he tipped into the arms of his father and Sally, who supported him on either side. Todd stood at a distance, uncomfortable but caring.

"I want to see Joyce," David said in a low voice.

"She's in intensive care," the doctor said. "Maybe tomorrow."

"I have to tell her . . ." He didn't know what.

"Time enough for that later," Nathan murmured,

holding David close and stroking his hair. "It wasn't your fault, son."

But David knew better.

The four of them got into Sally's station wagon and drove home, with Mister T sleeping in his crate in the back. David couldn't bear to look at him.

"Max?" he said once.

Nathan's arm tightened around him. "He's dead."

"I killed him."

"Yes. You had to. He'd have killed you."

Tears poured down David's face then, over the bandage on his cheek. "He was my dog. He loved me. I loved him."

"Honey," Sally said, gripping David's knee, "at that instant he was insane. He didn't know who or what he was attacking."

"But why. . . ?"

No one answered. They rode silently.

"Your class," David said, suddenly remembering.

Sally shrugged. "Not important."

"You tried to tell me," David said, twisting toward the woman.

"Never mind about that now. We can talk about it later."

David nodded and became aware that he hurt. His left cheek was burning, and there was another sore, bandaged place on his collarbone. He touched the bandages.

"He bit you a couple of times," Nathan said quietly. "We tried to get to you, get him off you. It just happened so fast, son. If you hadn't had that arrow in your hand . . ."

93

I might be dead, David thought. The realization washed over him like ice water.

Turning the corner onto their street they almost collided with Natalie's little Subaru. She saw them and braked, and flung herself out of the car to peer in through Sally's window.

"David? Thank God. I just got home and there was all that blood, and one of the Bates kids told me what happened. Are you all right? Nate, why didn't you call me?"

"He's okay," Nathan said. "Just a couple of superficial bite wounds. I didn't have the number where you were, and I couldn't remember Julie's last name, to look it up at the hospital."

Natalie got back into her car and did a swift U-turn to follow them home. Near their driveway lay a black mound. David couldn't look at Max.

As they all got out of the cars, Nathan said to Natalie, "Here, hon, take David inside. I'll take care of this."

Sally drove off, Todd picked up his bike and bow and silently pedaled away. David allowed his mother to lead him into the house, while Nathan approached the black form at the curb.

12

A few weeks later, on a crisp Saturday morning in October, David sat on the back steps staring at the dog run, along the garage wall. He thought, *I'll knock it down. Today. I can't stand to look at it any longer.*

He had been avoiding looking at it since Max's death. He avoided looking at the mound of earth at the back of the yard, where Nathan had buried Max, and he never looked at the collar and leash that still hung by the back door.

David felt a need this morning to take down the run, to have it over with once and for all. Joyce was home from the hospital. She had years of plastic surgery ahead of her to rebuild the damage done to her face and throat, and David sickened at the thought of her. The lawsuit proceeded, between the two families' insurance companies; Nathan never talked about that in front of David, but he knew it was going on.

Sometimes David woke in the morning and stretched his feet toward Max's bulky warmth, before he remembered.

Max was gone. Killed by David, who loved him.

Now David felt a need to tear the run down and get it out of his sight. A few days after the accident Nathan had suggested to David that a new dog might be a good idea, maybe one of Sally's Goldens. The temptation was a hard pull inside David, but he knew he dared not take that responsibility again. He had killed Corky with neglect, killed Max by stabbing him with an arrow. No, not another dog.

And so, the run must come down. Looking at the diamond pattern of the chain link mesh, David remembered the happiness with which he and his father had built the run, so few months ago. He ached.

"There you are," a voice said behind him. He turned and saw Sally and one of her dogs rounding the corner of the house. "I knocked at the front. Nobody heard me."

"Nobody's home," David said, but he was glad to see her. He looked down at the dog and recognized Bear. The dog galumphed into David's arms and gave him the love he gave to everyone, openhanded.

Sally made a shove-over motion with her hip, and settled beside David on the step. "You haven't been out to see us in a while, old Bear and I figured we better come and see you."

"No shows this weekend?" David asked, not really caring. That world was no longer his.

"Got one tomorrow, just over to Oskaloosa, no overnight trip. Why don't you ride along? Mister T ought to finish his CD title tomorrow if he doesn't get to clowning around and blow it again like he did at Green Bay."

David shrugged, "Nah, I don't think so. Thanks."

"How long you planning to sit around here and pout?"

"I'm not pouting," David flared.

96

"All right. Feeling sorry for yourself then. Whatever."

David glowered at her. "You came to cheer me up,
didn't you?" he accused.

"Yes. So shoot me. Come on"—she punched his
leg—"are you going to trip over your chin forever?"

"Probably." But a smile was fighting through.

"Listen," Sally said. "I didn't come here just to cheer
you up. I came to make you a business proposition."

"What's that?"

"I need to farm Bear out on a co-ownership. You're
the only person I know that I'd trust with him."

"Farm him out? What do you mean?" In spite of himself David felt a flare of interest. Bear had finished sniffing his way around the yard, and had found a stick for
David to throw for him. David threw it.

"You know. Farm him out on co-ownership, like I do
with my older dogs. I told you about how I do that with
my brood bitches after I'm through using them for
breeding. I find a good pet home for them, give them
away on a co-ownership basis, the dog gets to retire in
comfort, and I get kennel space for the next generation.
That way I can keep upgrading my quality without getting overloaded with senior citizen dogs, and the families get great pets, champions, for nothing."

"Yes, but Bear," David said. "I never thought you'd
do that with Bear. He's your stud dog. He's so special."

Sally shook her head. "I know that, dummy. I never
thought I'd find anybody I'd let have old Bear. I figured
he'd be with me till he went to Golden heaven. But
now I've got this Mister T dog coming up. Did I tell
you he finished his championship?"

97

"No, did he really?" David grinned for the first time in weeks.

Sally glowed. "Took him to that Des Moines circuit two weeks ago, three all-breed shows and a golden retriever specialty. He was Winners Dog at the specialty, got five points for that, and then he got two four-point wins at the all-breed shows, and finished the next weekend at Rochester. How's that for style?"

"Fantastic," David said, and he meant it.

"So," Sally went on, "I've definitely decided to keep him for breeding. In fact I've got two outside bitches coming in this fall, from people that saw him at the specialty. And I really don't have kennel space for more than one stud dog, plus visiting bitches. You'd be doing me a favor, taking Bear. You've got a nice run there, going to waste, and besides . . ."

David understood. "You think I need a dog, to get me over Max."

She nodded.

"I've already killed both of the dogs I've had," he said from the depths of his unhappiness. "You'd be crazy to trust me with your champion-UDT-Obedience Champion stud dog."

"Trust you? Why wouldn't I? I don't know another kid your age that takes his responsibilities as seriously as you do."

"Sally," he argued, "I just told you. I killed Max and I killed Corky. What do you want from me?"

"You didn't kill Max, you dumb kid," she said wearily. "That was done to him long before you came along."

"What do you mean?"

She sighed. "Whoever it was that took that dog and

attack trained him, brainwashed him to the point where he could go off half-cocked like he did that night, that's who killed him. And everybody before that, that bred Max and his ancestors with the goal of producing dogs with such hair-trigger aggression that their sanity was in danger even without the attack training. David, if you hadn't killed Max when you did you could be dead yourself right now."

"I know that," he muttered. "It doesn't really help."

"Also," she went on, "supposing you'd just pulled him off of that little girl and left it at that, supposing you'd been able to. He would have died anyway, David. He was under probation already, under the one-bite law. He'd have been officially put to death for attacking Joyce, whether you'd done anything or not. And he should have been. There was no way that dog could have been allowed to live without his being a constant threat to the people around him."

David knew it was true.

Sally wrapped her arm around his shoulder. "Look at it this way. Max had, what, six months of extra life because of you, which he wouldn't have had if you hadn't taken him on. He enjoyed those six months, and so did you."

"Yeah, and Joyce Bates has to pay for it," David muttered.

Sally sighed and bumped him against her in a hard hug. "You did what you could. And about Corky, from what you told me about her, you can't blame yourself for that, David. I used to do a lot of pet grooming before the Canine Castle opened up in the mall. I used to see the most horribly matted dogs coming in all the time. Cockers, poodles, Shih Tzus, and Lhasas, they were the worst. No. Old English sheepdogs, they were the worst. I'd have to shave them down to the skin all over, and I'd tell their owners how to comb them so they wouldn't get matted again, and next time here would come the same dogs back again, matted to the eyeballs. Most pet owners simply don't groom their dogs. People who would never think of letting their children go uncombed for months do exactly that with their dogs."

David remembered Corky, and shuddered.

"But my point is, David, now I think your parents are lovely people and I'm not knocking them, but they had unrealistic expectations, handing a cocker spaniel to a little boy with no idea that puppies even needed to be combed. You didn't know what to do, you didn't have the right equipment to do it with, it was just plain too much to expect of you. And if you don't mind my saying so, they were wrong to take the dog away from you for that reason, especially when she ended up being put to sleep. That's a terrible load of guilt to dump on a little kid."

They sat silent and thoughtful for a long time. It was tempting, David thought. He bent down and ran his fingers up Bear's chest, combing the pale coat into spikes and twists. His logical mind told him that this made sense, taking Bear. There would be no savagery with this dog, not even a grooming problem. No reason to be afraid of the responsibility.

But he was afraid. It had cost him so much to love Corky, to love Max. He didn't know if he could do it again. He didn't know if he wanted to do it again. Easier to tear down the run and go without a dog. The

100

world was full of people who didn't have dogs. They got along just fine.

A hardening began inside David. He shook his head and looked away from Bear and Sally. "I don't want him. I don't really like dogs all that much. You better take him on home now."

Glancing at Sally's face he saw a flicker of hurt. It startled him. He hadn't known he had the power to hurt this tough middle-aged woman.

She stood up. "Okay, if you really feel that way. I'm not going to push him on you. Come on, Bear, let's go."

David opened his mouth to say no, he didn't mean it, he wanted Bear. But she was already out of sight around the corner. Just as well, he told himself. He hung on to the hardening inside himself. It wasn't strong enough to be trusted yet, and he needed it.

13

A few minutes later Nathan came around the corner of the house carrying a bag of groceries. His voice seemed painfully loud and brisk against David's mood.

"What was Sally doing here? We just about had a fender bender at the corner. She looked upset, or mad or something. What happened?"

David got up abruptly and went into the garage for the hammer, to start taking down the run.

"Nothing."

"Nothing? She was here to see you, wasn't she? What'd she have to say?"

"Nothing."

Nathan stared at David over the top of the grocery bag, his face soft with concern. But when David turned his back and began clawing fence staples out of a corner post with the hammer, Nathan eased away, maneuvering through the back door with his armload.

During lunch the phone rang; Todd called to tell David that the straw-bale archery target was finally built and ready to try out. David said no thanks, he didn't feel like coming over.

"You should have gone," Natalie said as David returned to his spaghetti. "You don't have anything else to do this afternoon, do you?"

David shrugged. "I got the fence wire all taken down, and the gate off. I was going to dig out the corner posts this afternoon."

Nathan and Natalie exchanged looks. "No hurry about that job, is there?" Nathan asked. David shrugged.

After a silent moment, Nathan said, "I know what let's do this afternoon. Let's all of us go down to the marina and see what they've got for sale in the way of fishing boats. Want to?"

David looked up, suspicious. "How come you've got the hots for a fishing boat all of a sudden?"

"Not so sudden," Nathan said. "We've talked about it before."

"Just talked. I didn't think you really wanted one."

Natalie said, "I can't this afternoon. I've got that discussion group over at Norma's. I told you about that."

Nathan looked intently at David. "Come on, be a normal kid. What normal kid wouldn't want to go shopping for a fishing boat on a great Saturday afternoon like this? Come on, humor your old man."

"Well, if we're going to pretend to be *normal* . . ." David slipped into the old easy teasing, surprised at the pleasure it gave his father.

After lunch David settled comfortably into his father's car, glad in spite of himself for the distraction of boat shopping, and the delay in the tearing down of the dog run. It had been harder than he'd imagined it would be, ripping down the memories of his dreams for

103

Max, the happiness with which he and Nathan had built the run.

They drove north out of town, past Sally's house, where David looked, in spite of himself, for a glimpse of her. They turned left onto a winding blacktop road that led between rustic sprawling homes with small attractive stables and riding arenas. The road curled and dipped through the hills and finally emerged on a high ridge overlooking the dam and reservoir lying deep and glistening in the valley below.

Nathan swung the car into a landscaped scenic overlook and coasted to a stop. They rolled down their windows, leaned arms along the opened edges, and breathed in the early autumn scents of forest and lake.

"What are we stopping for, as if I didn't know," David asked darkly.

"We have to talk about this boat thing. We have to figure out how much we can afford to spend, and how big a boat we need, before we walk into the hands of a high-pressure boat salesman." Nathan smiled, his eyes telling David that no one was fooling anyone here.

"Come off it, Dad. You don't really want a boat. If you'd really wanted a fishing boat we'd have had one before this. Heck, you go fishing maybe once every five years, tops."

"That's true, but if it would help get your mind off Max, it'd be a good investment."

"I figured that's what this was all about."

Nathan wiggled down into a more comfortable position around the steering column, and laid his head back against the headrest. "You want to tell me what Sally wanted this morning?"

"Nothing."

"Yes she did. She called me about it at the office yesterday. She wanted to give you one of her dogs, didn't she?"

"Not give. Farm out on a co-ownership. She does that a lot with her older dogs. Well, you already know all about that if you and she were talking about it behind my back already." David bristled, but not much.

"She just wanted to be sure it would be all right with me and your mom before she made you the proposition. She did right, don't get all defensive about it."

"I'm not. I just didn't want Bear."

"He's a nice dog. It'd be kind of fun to have a dog with all those championships and titles."

"You want me to take him, don't you? Why don't you just say so? We don't have to go through all this boat crap."

Quietly Nathan said, "What I want is for you to want the dog yourself, not just take him because I want you to."

David crossed his leg and picked at the loose sole of his tennis shoe. "How come you want me to have him? What difference does it make to you?"

"Well," Nathan drew the word out thoughtfully, "maybe I want you to have Bear for the same reason you wanted to have Max."

David scowled. "That doesn't make any sense."

"Sure it does. You wanted Max because you felt guilty about messing up with Corky. I want you to have Bear, because I feel so guilty about your mom and me messing up with both situations, Corky and Max."

David squinted at him, puzzling it out.

"You're not the only guy in this situation who's got a load of responsibility around his neck, you know,"

105

Nathan said with a crooked smile. "The way you felt about your dogs, that's not a patch on the kind of responsibility I feel for you. And the way you loved those dogs isn't even a fraction of the way I feel about you."

David looked down, silent with emotion.

Nathan went on. "Mom and I knew we screwed up the situation with Corky. We just plain expected too much of you when you were too little to handle it. That was our fault, not yours. And we didn't expect her to be put to sleep." His hand cupped the back of David's neck, and kneaded it. "We thought she'd go to a good home. And we shouldn't have let you know what did happen to her. Parents mess up sometimes, with the best of intentions."

David smiled stiffly and leaned his head back into his father's hand. "Yeah. So do kids."

Nathan plodded on. "Screw-up number two was that I should have had better sense than to let you take on that Doberman. All these years your mom and I were kind of waiting for you to ask for another dog. Hoping you would. We were scared we'd done you some real damage, with Corky."

David looked up then, looked fully at his father. "You talked about that, you and Mom? You worried about it?"

The hand gripped his neck and shook it. "Don't sound so happy. Worrying about what you might have done to your kid is not one of the fun aspects of parenthood, let me tell you."

David tipped his head back again, his grin widening.

"What I was getting at," Nathan continued, "is that if I'd had the brains of a rock I'd never have let you take on Max. That was a dangerous situation from the word go, and I don't mind admitting I was scared of that dog. And terrified that you were going to get hurt by him."

"Then why? How come you let me keep him?"

Nathan shrugged and withdrew his hand. "Trying to feel my way through the dark labyrinth of fatherhood."

Through the silence came faraway sounds of motorboats on the reservoir below.

David said, "But how come it's so important to you that I take Bear? Why don't we just give up on dogs? Get me a nice gerbil or something?"

"Because you do love dogs, Davie. I know you. You're closer to me than anyone in my life has ever been. When you were little and got upset stomachs, I used to throw up, too. Did you know that?"

"You did not," David scoffed, looking from the corner of his eye.

"Well, not all the time, but sometimes. And I know you love dogs. It just shines out of you every time you're around one. So that means that if you shy away from taking Bear, who is the perfect dog for you, that means that Mom and I have done damage to you, see? I don't want to have damaged you."

Nathan's voice strained around a tightened throat, and David's throat ached in response.

"So in other words," he said, "I'm a rotten kid if I don't take Bear, so you don't have to feel guilty about me anymore, right?"

"Only if you really want the dog," Nathan said in a saintly tone.

"You know what, Dad?"

"What?"

"I bet you end up a rich lawyer with carpet on your

107

office floor after all. You can talk anybody into anything."

Nathan laughed in pure bubbling relief.

"Hey, Dad, are we going to go buy that fishing boat now?"

"What fishing boat? What do I want with a boat? I go fishing maybe once every five years, remember?"

As Nathan turned the ignition key David said, "Hey, want to help me build a dog run this afternoon?

"You're not an entirely rotten kid."

"You're not an entirely rotten dad. Except you won't buy me a fishing boat."

"Get out of here, creep. And get your shoes off the dashboard."

They laughed together, and turned toward home.